Calloway County Public Library

Lindberg, Becky Thom
Speak up, Chelsea Ma
3288000149254

P9-BXX-149

J
Lind   Lindberg, Becky Thoman

        Speak up, Chelsea Martin!

                            081292

Calloway County Public Library
710 Main Street
Murray, KY 42071

1. Books may be kept two weeks and may be renewed once
for the same period, except 7 day books and magazines.

2. A fine is charged for each day a book is not returned according to the above rule. No book will be issued to any person in-
curring such a fine until it has been paid.

3. All injuries to books beyond reasonable wear and all
losses shall be made good to the satisfaction of the Librarian.

4. Each borrower is held responsible for all books charged
on his card and for all fines accruing on the same.

Speak Up,
Chelsea Martin!

Speak Up, Chelsea Martin!

BECKY THOMAN LINDBERG

Illustrations by NANCY POYDAR

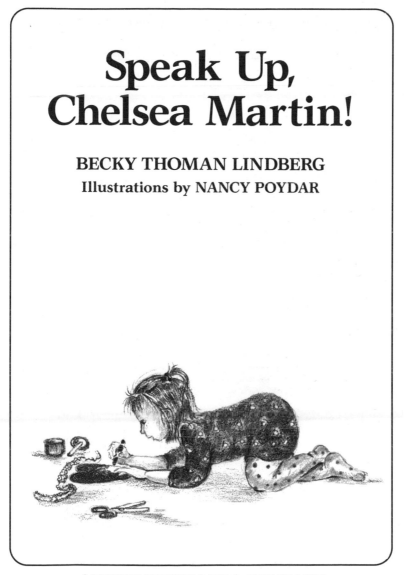

ALBERT WHITMAN & COMPANY
Morton Grove, Illinois

Text © 1991 by Becky Thoman Lindberg.
Illustrations © 1991 by Nancy Poydar.
Designed by Susan B. Cohn.
Published in 1991 by Albert Whitman & Company,
6340 Oakton Street, Morton Grove, Illinois 60053-2723.
Published simultaneously in Canada by
General Publishing, Limited, Toronto.
All rights reserved. Printed in U.S.A.
10 9 8 7 6 5 4 3 2 1

Library of Congress Cataloging-in-Publication Data

Lindberg, Becky Thoman.
    Speak up, Chelsea Martin! / Becky Thoman Lindberg;
illustrated by Nancy Poydar.
        p.   cm.
    Summary: Third-grader Chelsea Martin deals with
a bully, has a fight with her best friend, and learns
to speak up.
    ISBN 0-8075-7552-6
        [1. Friendship—Fiction.] I. Poydar, Nancy, ill.
II. Title.
PZ7.L65716Sp   1991
[Fic]—dc20   91-313
                                         CIP
                                          AC

B+T – 8-11-92

To my daughter, Carolyn Lindberg.

Contents

···1···

A Mushy Mess

Mary Lynne was an almost perfect best friend, Chelsea Martin thought. Almost perfect, but not quite.

It was eight-thirty on a cool morning in early November. As usual, Chelsea was walking to school with Mary Lynne. And, as usual, Mary Lynne was doing all the talking.

She talks too much, Chelsea said to herself. She held onto her backpack shoulder strap with one hand and stuck the other hand deep in the pocket of her denim jacket.

And that wasn't all. It sometimes seemed to Chelsea that Mary Lynne always got her way. But

Chelsea couldn't ever say that to Mary Lynne. What if she got angry?

Now Mary Lynne held her arm in front of Chelsea's nose. "Look what I got this weekend!" A bracelet made of colored beads circled her wrist.

"The white beads spell my name, M-A-R-Y, see? I looked for a bracelet with 'Chelsea' on it, but there wasn't one."

Mary Lynne stopped to take a breath and then chattered on.

After a while Chelsea gave up trying to listen. She just stared at Mary Lynne's mouth. Words were flowing out of it in a steady stream. Chelsea squinted—she could almost see them.

Wouldn't it be funny, she thought, if the words somehow turned into rubber balls?

Pop! Bounce! Pop! Bounce! Pop! Bounce! Red balls, blue balls, yellow balls—all tumbling out of Mary Lynne's mouth. Chelsea giggled.

"What?" demanded Mary Lynne. "I didn't say anything funny."

"Nothing," murmured Chelsea. "I was just . . .thinking."

Mary Lynne gave her a questioning look, then shrugged and said, "Mrs. Findlay's been giving us too much homework. Don't you think so?"

Chelsea opened her mouth, but Mary Lynne went on without waiting for an answer.

Again Chelsea half-closed her eyes. She pictured herself catching three of the word balls, then juggling them. Up, up, up they'd go, into the crisp November air.

By now the girls had reached the edge of the school grounds. Glancing at her wristwatch, Mary Lynne said, "So I thought . . . hey, look over there!"

Mary Lynne pointed toward a small group of girls, third graders like themselves. They were all staring at something lying on the ground near the sandbox. Mary Lynne and Chelsea ran over to join the others.

The thing on the ground was a doll, Chelsea realized. Someone had brought a Barbie doll to school. But something was wrong. Puzzled, she stepped closer.

Over the doll's bathing suit was a flowered wraparound skirt. A string of blossoms hung

Calloway County Public Library
710 Main Street
Murray, KY   42071

around her neck. Above the neck there was—nothing!

Island Fun Barbie had lost her head.

"How did it happen?" whispered Chelsea.

Katie Klein pushed her blonde bangs off her forehead and shrugged. "Nobody knows. Paula put it down for just a minute, and when she came back..."

Paula sat slumped on the edge of the sandbox. Fat tears dripped from her eyes, slid down her cheeks, and soaked into the sand.

Chelsea shivered. Who would do such an awful thing? Wrapping her arms around herself, she looked up at the sky. Was it her imagination? Or was it getting colder?

A mound of dark clouds, like charcoal-colored Cool Whip, had piled up right above the school. There was something strange about those clouds.

Then she noticed the pine trees behind the playground. Their branches whipped back and forth, back and forth, as if a huge, invisible hand were shaking them.

She knew in her heart there was nothing to be

afraid of. Even so, Chelsea was filled with a delicious feeling of terror. "I know who did it," she whispered to Mary Lynne. "Maybe it was some kind of monster!"

"Monster!" said Mary Lynne scornfully. "This is no time to be playing games. We have to find out what really happened!"

Chelsea felt hurt. "I wasn't—"

"Hey! Hey, everybody!" Beverly Ann ran toward the group of girls, shouting and waving her arms. She staggered to a stop in front of the sandbox. "They're over by the basketball court! And they've got Barbie's head!"

"Who?" Several girls spoke at once. "Who took it?"

Beverly Ann smoothed her long, blonde hair. She glanced around to make sure she had everyone's attention. "The fifth-grade boys! That's who!"

The girls looked at each other. Uh-oh, thought Chelsea.

If there was anything Chelsea couldn't stand, it was a fifth-grade boy. Oh, there were a few she admired. But on the whole—yuck!

She pictured them barging through the school grounds. Then they changed from a group of boys into something else: a snorting, stamping herd of...cattle, that was it! Tiny red eyes glaring, nostrils flaring, hooves pawing the ground!

The picture vanished as someone demanded, "Well, what are we going to do about it?"

It was Lucy Burnett, who had more courage than the other third-grade girls. She actually had a *brother* in fifth grade. Chelsea figured that Lucy got practice fighting at home.

Now Chelsea looked around at the excited faces of her friends. Even Paula was on her feet, clutching her headless Barbie doll.

"Let's go after them!" cried Lucy.

Again the girls looked at each other.

Mary Lynne's eyes sparkled. "Yeah!" she said. "Let's get Barbie's head back!"

Chelsea was impressed. She hadn't realized that Mary Lynne was so brave. She herself didn't feel brave at all.

Chelsea's mother, who worked in the service

department of a local car dealership, was always reminding Chelsea to be assertive.

"Don't let people trample all over you," she would say, after a day of dealing with unhappy customers. "Stay calm, be polite, but stand up for yourself."

Remembering her mother's words, Chelsea straightened her back.

"Come on," said Lucy. "Let's go."

In a tightly packed bunch, they moved across the playground. They headed toward the fifth-grade boys' hangout, the old basketball court.

Chelsea had made sure she was in the center of the bunch, where she wouldn't be noticed.

In front, Lucy moved forward, a determined look on her face. "We want Barbie's head!" she called out, as if she were leading a cheer.

Mary Lynne grinned at Chelsea and repeated, "We want Barbie's head!"

Soon they were all chanting it. Chelsea found herself shouting, "Barbie's head! Barbie's head!" along with everybody else.

The girls marched across the playground. But

as they came closer to the basketball court, their footsteps slowed. Ahead was a group of five or six boys. They stood in a loose circle, laughing and tossing a small ball to each other.

No. It wasn't a ball. It was...

"Look!" cried Paula indignantly. "They're playing catch with my Barbie's head!"

Lucy came to a sudden stop, and the other girls piled up behind her.

"Hey, look who's here!" called out Billy Burnett. "It's my sister and her little friends." He stuck out his tongue. "Scram, you creepy girls! Beat it!"

But Lucy took a deep breath. "You took the head off Paula's Barbie doll. You'd better give it back!"

"Oh, yeah? Who's gonna make us?"

"Get lost!" called another boy.

Lucy stamped her foot. "I'll tell Mom if you don't give it back!"

There, thought Chelsea. They'll have to give it back now. She was shocked when the boys began to laugh.

"Oooooh, don't do that!" said Billy Burnett, pretending to cringe. Then he laughed his annoying laugh. "Heh, heh, heh!"

"Wait a minute, she's right," said Ronald Crinks. "We *should* give it back."

Chelsea stared at him in surprise. Then she saw the wink he gave the other boys.

"Oh, yeah, we'll give it back."

"Sure we will." Billy Burnett stepped forward a few paces.

"The question is," said Ronald, who was also moving forward in a threatening way, "what are you going to give us?"

As the boys moved toward them, the girls backed up, inch by inch. Taking a step without looking behind her, Chelsea stumbled over something. It was a backpack.

Her foot had pressed on something soft, too soft to be a book. It would be terrible, she thought, if she had stepped on someone's lunch.

She looked up and caught Ronald Crinks staring at her. He stuck out his tongue and then laughed in his nasty way.

Oh! He made her feel so small, like something that crawled out of a hole. A...a...worm! That's what.

She seemed to hear her mother saying, "Speak up for yourself, Chelsea!" And she thought of Lucy, brave enough to face fifth-grade boys.

I will not be a worm, Chelsea told herself. She stood up straight.

An idea popped into her head. Glancing around, she saw that a number of the boys' backpacks had been dumped carelessly on the ground. Just a few feet away, in fact, was a gray bag with the name *Burnett* written in large letters on the front zipper pocket.

Chelsea set her own backpack down and took a step closer to the one belonging to Billy.

She pounced on it!

She dragged the bag into the circle of girls. Looking up triumphantly, she saw Billy Burnett glaring at her.

"Hey, what're you doing with my backpack?"

By this time, Chelsea had pulled a red plastic lunchbox out of the pack. Keeping her eyes on

Billy, she fumbled open the catch and groped inside.

Her heart pounded with excitement. Her fingers closed on something—a banana! Perfect!

She blurted out the words before she could lose her nerve. "This is what we'll give you—Billy's lunch! You can have it back when you give us the Barbie head."

Chelsea could hear a surprised murmur coming from the other girls.

From the boys, there arose a low growling sound. Now they did not seem like a herd of cattle. They were more like a pack of wolves, ready to close in on a helpless victim.

"You hand that over right now," said Billy Burnett, scowling. He lunged forward, his hands held out as if to grab Chelsea.

"Better not!" warned Ronald Crinks. "Mr. Marella and Mrs. Findlay are right over there!" He pointed toward the back door of the school.

Chelsea glanced at her teacher. Mrs. Findlay was facing the other way, chatting to the principal. But just knowing that the two of them were within calling distance made Chelsea feel braver.

She held up the banana. In a quivery voice she said, "One more step and your banana turns into SQUASH!"

"The little twerp wouldn't dare!" called out Ronald.

Now Chelsea felt more angry than afraid. Twerp, huh? She'd show them!

"This is your last chance. Give back that Barbie head or else!"

"Ha! Ha!" responded Ronald. He bent over double, pretending to be overcome by laughter. The other boys took the cue. They poked each other in the ribs and acted as if they just couldn't stop laughing.

All right! Chelsea said to herself. I'll do it! I really will. She dashed the piece of fruit to the ground.

The boys stopped laughing. Everyone watched with big eyes as Chelsea held her foot three inches above the banana.

Behind her, Mary Lynne whispered, "Go ahead."

Down came Chelsea's foot. STAMP!
S-Q-U-A-S-H went the banana. Yellow goo oozed
out of the burst skin.

"Yuck!" murmured someone. Everyone stared
in silence at the mushy mess on the ground.
Chelsea wiped the bottom of her shoe.

"I'm glad!" muttered Lucy. She glared at her
brother. "He deserved it."

Chelsea reached into Billy's lunchbox and
pulled out a bag of potato chips. She waved it in
the air. "*Now* will you give us back Barbie's
head?"

Five angry boys stared at her. "Never!" cried
Ronald Crinks.

But Chelsea noticed that Billy Burnett did not
look happy. "Not my potato chips," he moaned.

Chelsea waved the bag back and forth. "This
is your last chance to save them."

Billy set his lips in a thin line, crossed his arms,
and shook his head.

Chelsea smiled. She held the bag of potato chips
gently in the palm of her hand. She could feel
everyone's eyes on her.

Suddenly—CRUNCH—she closed her fingers and ground the chips into crumbs. Holding the lunchbox under her arm, she opened the top of the bag. She turned it upside-down and shook.

A shower of crumbs drifted to the earth. Chelsea ground them into the blacktop.

A groan rose up from the boys.

Chelsea peeked into the red lunchbox. Only one thing left. She held up a thick peanut butter and jelly sandwich.

"Wait a minute!" In a sad voice Billy said, "I give up." He reached into his pants pocket and took out the head of Island Fun Barbie.

"Hey! Don't!" protested Ronald.

"It's *my* lunch," said Billy. "And I didn't have any breakfast. If she smashes my sandwich, I'll starve to death."

"Can't you buy lunch? Don't you have any money?"

Billy nodded. "Sure, but it's 'meat loaf surprise' today, remember? I can't eat *that*!"

"Here, you can have your old doll's head back!" He tossed the Barbie head in the air. It landed in some bushes, and Paula ran to search for it.

Chelsea shoved the sandwich back into the lunchbox just as the bell rang. She left the lunchbox on the ground next to Billy's backpack and walked quickly toward the school entrance.

As she hurried toward the school door, her friends crowded around her, laughing and talking excitedly. Now Mary Lynne was impressed. "I can't believe you did that, Chelsea!"

Chelsea was pleased by all the attention. Only one little thing bothered her—Billy Burnett's words as he stooped to pick up what was left of his lunch.

"Watch out, Chelsea Martin! You'd better just *watch out*!"

...2...

A Noise in the Night

"I'm writing a play," Chelsea said, plopping herself down at the small, white kitchen table.

She spread her loose-leaf binder out in front of her. From behind her ear she took a pencil. It was a silly place to keep a pencil, but she had seen a reporter on television do it. If she was going to be a writer, she wanted to look the part.

"A play?" said Chelsea's mother. "That's nice. What kind of play?"

"Um..." Chelsea thought it over. "A Thanksgiving play."

After all, Thanksgiving was only ten days away. If the play was good enough, Mrs. Findlay might let the class perform it in school.

Dreamily, Chelsea rested her chin on the palm of her hand. She would write parts for everyone. Let's see...Mary Lynne would like a part with lots of talking. She could be the narrator.

And Lucy had lent Chelsea her new box of crayons yesterday; she should have a good part. Maybe she could be the turkey.

Chelsea bent over her paper. *Act I, Scene I,* she printed. She touched the pencil eraser to her tongue. A title was what she needed now.

"How does this sound?" Chelsea asked, turning to her mother. "*The Revenge of the Turkey.*"

Mrs. Martin stood in front of the refrigerator, staring into the freezer compartment. "Hmmm?" She held up two rock-hard packages of food for Chelsea to see. "Which of these do you want—Salisbury steak with gravy or pepperoni pizza?"

"Pizza, I guess. But what do you think about the title? *Revenge of the Turkey?* Or how about *The Turkey That Bulldozed Baltimore?*"

Chelsea's mother set the timer on the microwave. "Well," she said thoughtfully, pushing a strand of brown hair behind her ear, "I guess I like the way *The Turkey That Bulldozed Baltimore* sounds. Except...we live pretty close to Baltimore, you know. Bulldozing the city seems a little unfriendly."

She took a carton of milk out of the refrigerator. "Maybe it should be *The Turkey That Saved Baltimore.*"

"'Hmmm—I'll think about it." Chelsea began to write slowly and carefully in cursive.

"Okay. But Chelsea," reminded her mother, "don't forget your homework!"

After dinner Chelsea helped her mother put the plates and silverware into the dishwasher. "My play's almost done," she said, as she wiped off the table with a yellow sponge.

Half an hour later she had finished the last page. "Can I call Dad and tell him about it?" she asked her mother.

Chelsea's parents had been divorced for two years now. Last year her father had moved out of town. Chelsea visited him in the summer and sometimes on holidays. But not too often, because airplane tickets were expensive.

Mrs. Martin glanced at the clock. "All right, but don't talk long. You haven't started your homework yet, have you?"

Mr. Martin answered the telephone on the first ring. When Chelsea told him about the play, he sounded pleased. "What's the title?"

"*The Turkey That Saved Baltimore*. It's about a turkey who *was* going to bulldoze Baltimore because he was mad at everybody. But then a big fire started, and he didn't want the whole city to be burned up."

Chelsea wound the telephone cord around her finger. "So he put out the fire. And then he was the star of the Thanksgiving parade!"

"Sounds good!" said Mr. Martin. "Send me a copy of it, okay honey?"

"Sure, Dad." Smiling happily, Chelsea tucked her pencil behind her ear. She decided to add a few details to the ending to make the play even better. Taking her loose-leaf binder, she went upstairs to her bedroom to work on it.

After a while, she heard her mother calling. "It's eight o'clock, Chelsea! Time for your bath."

"Okay, Mom." On her way to the linen closet to get a towel, Chelsea thought of something. Homework! She still had to do homework. Well, she'd do it later, after her bath.

As she was about to step into the tub, she remembered her beauty treatment. Ah, there it was, in the medicine cabinet over the sink. *Marvelous Mud Mask*.

Once a week her mother used it on her face. To remove dead cells, she said.

Chelsea didn't know exactly why the cells died. But if the mud mask got rid of *them*, it might just work on freckles. She'd been using it once a week, just like her mother, but so far...

She shook the tube, then squeezed it. A gloppy blob of green stuff dropped into her palm.

The first time she'd done this, she had been surprised to discover that the Marvelous Mud Mask was not really mud. Instead, it looked like bits of green sand mixed with lime-flavored Kool-Aid.

She smoothed it on her nose and cheeks. By

the end of her bath, the mask would become dry and hard. She would have to scrub it off with her washcloth.

Then, standing in front of the mirror, she would peer hopefully at her reflection. Maybe this time would be different. Always before, the same old face with the same old freckles had stared back at her.

And the same old bare ears. Chelsea had been wanting to have her ears pierced for a long time now.

She imagined herself wearing little gold hoops that would catch the light when she turned her head. But her mother always said, "Not yet," or "Maybe when you're older. Eight years is *too young*."

Chelsea thought her mother wouldn't mind if she got rid of the freckles. The scattered brown dots on Chelsea's nose and cheeks had appeared mysteriously two summers ago.

She didn't know why it had to happen to her. Mary Lynne didn't have freckles. Mary Lynne had lovely smooth skin, and it was just the color of

Mrs. Martin's favorite beverage—coffee with lots of milk.

Later, sitting in the tub with her knees drawn up to her chest and suds everywhere, Chelsea began to feel bored. She gave a little red plastic boat a poke with one finger. Really, she was too old for these bathtub toys.

She found the washcloth and began to scrub her arms. Funny, she thought, how a wet washcloth can stick to things.

She wound it around her arm like a cast. As she stretched out to admire the effect, she some-how knocked the bathmat from the side of the tub into the water.

Uh-oh! The bathmat sank immediately. Chelsea looked at it sadly; it was too soggy now to dry her feet on.

I might as well enjoy myself, she decided, wrapping the mat around her left leg. For a while she sat quietly in the tub with her right arm and her left leg held stiffly above the water. This is how I'd have to take a bath if I had plaster casts, she thought.

But it would really be hard to take a bath with a broken arm and *two* broken legs.

Chelsea reached out her left arm and grabbed the fluffy towel that she had set on a chair beside the tub. Now this was the hard part; she had to dunk the towel into the water and wrap it around her right leg, using her left arm only. Her right arm was still broken.

"Chelsea!" her mother called. "Are you still in the tub? You must be all shriveled up!"

Chelsea held out her hand. It was true. The tips of her fingers were almost white, and they were wrinkly. She'd better get out.

Quickly she scrubbed the Marvelous Mud Mask off her face. Then, after squeezing the washcloth, she hung it up.

She squeezed the bathmat and towel, too. But they were so big and heavy! And wet!

And that wasn't all. Too late, Chelsea saw that the towel she had taken from the linen closet was a fancy new one her mother had bought on sale— one she wanted to keep for company.

Now Chelsea was worried. So worried she

didn't even bother checking to see whether her freckles were gone.

What would her mother say about the new, soaking-wet towel? Chelsea didn't know, and she didn't want to find out.

When she was all dry and in her pajamas, she took another towel and wrapped the wet things in it. Then she carried the whole bundle into her room and stuffed it under her bed. When her mother wasn't around—maybe tomorrow when she was visiting Mrs. DeCastro next door—Chelsea would toss everything in the clothes dryer.

In the middle of the night, Chelsea woke up. She sat up with the covers pulled around her and rubbed her eyes.

Then she remembered. She'd had a bad dream. A dream about Billy Burnett. He'd been chasing her, and she'd been running...running...running, trying to get away. And then she tripped.

His hands had reached toward her, she started to yell—and she opened her eyes. She was awake.

Chelsea shivered a little. In the dream, Billy had seemed twice his normal size. Now she imagined him standing there in front of her, at the foot of the bed.

She wrinkled her nose. "I don't like you, Billy," she whispered. She didn't know how Lucy could *stand* having him for a brother!

Even before the Barbie doll episode, she hadn't approved of him. There was his hair, for one thing. Billy's hair stuck up all over the top of his head. Chelsea thought he looked like a cartoon character whose finger was caught in an electrical outlet.

Then there was his annoying laugh, high and shrill—heh, heh, heh!

But the worst thing was—ugh!—the rabbit's foot. A real fur-covered rabbit's foot dangled by a chain from Billy's belt. And he wore it always.

Chelsea didn't care if a rabbit's foot *was* supposed to be lucky. She never saw it without feeling sorry for the poor bunny.

She had been worrying about Billy ever since the lunchbox incident. She had tried to keep out of his way. . . .

But once, when a line of fifth graders passed her in the hallway, Billy raised his fist and shook it in her direction. He had not forgotten about her—or forgiven her.

Somehow, things seemed worse in the middle of the night. What exactly did Billy have in mind? she wondered, when he said, "You'd better *watch out*!"

Chelsea shivered again.

Something else was bothering her—what? Uh-oh. She remembered the wet bundle under her bed. What if her mother discovered the towels before Chelsea had a chance to dry them?

Chelsea remembered the time she had dropped a wet bathing suit into the bottom of the clothes hamper and then stuffed other things in on top of it. A week later, when her mother finally did the wash, the bathing suit was covered with black spots—mildew.

If her mother found the new towel all smelly and covered with black spots, then she would be really angry. Chelsea decided to dry everything right now.

She climbed out of bed, got the little pink flashlight she kept in her nightstand, and gathered up the soggy towels and damp bathmat.

The washer and dryer were downstairs, in a tiny area off the kitchen. Chelsea stuffed the towels into the dryer and set the dial for "time dry."

Well, that ought to do it, she thought, feeling much better. She would take the towels out in the morning.

On her way back upstairs, she noticed her backpack lying on the floor near the front door. It was right where she'd left it after school. She had never done her homework!

What would happen if she went to school without it? Chelsea imagined herself sitting at her desk. "All right, class," Mrs. Findlay would say. "It's time for math."

Everyone would get out the homework papers. Everyone except Chelsea.

Then Mrs. Findlay would walk to the blackboard, jingling the gold bracelets she always wore. "Chelsea Martin," she'd say, "what is the answer to number one?"

Chelsea pictured herself trying to figure out the problem in her head while Mrs. Findlay waited.

No, she thought, it wouldn't work. She was pretty good at math, but not that good. She would have to do her homework now.

The townhouse was dark and cold. Chelsea switched on the table lamp and settled herself in a corner of the living room sofa. The afghan made a cozy covering for her legs. Now, for problem number one.

Third grade was doing multiplication, and Chelsea thought it was sort of fun. But somehow doing multiplication in the middle of the night was not fun. She had trouble keeping her mind on the work.

The problem: nine times nine. Chelsea wrote the answer: eighty-one. There...she had number one done. Then two.

But as she bent over the paper to start the third problem, she heard a strange noise. Whoo-o-oo! There it was again! She looked up quickly. What *was* that noise? And what was that shadow over in the corner?

Chelsea pulled the afghan over her head. She held her breath. Was it a monster? A ghost?

With her eyes squeezed shut, she began to count to herself. If something doesn't grab me by the time I reach ten, she decided, I'm safe.

One. . .two. . .three. . .

Ten long seconds went by. Chelsea pulled down a corner of the afghan and peeked out. Well. . .how about that? Nothing there.

Then Chelsea heard the noise again. Whoo-o-oo! Whoo-o-oo! Where was it coming from?

She looked over at the window. The branches of the little pine tree outside were beating against the glass. It must be awfully windy out there. Oh, that was the noise—just the wind!

The world outdoors was black, and the window was beaded with raindrops. A perfect night to snuggle under the bedcovers.

Chelsea sighed. Since there was no monster, she supposed she would have to do her homework after all. She read the next math problem.

In a little while, she yawned and put down her pencil. She counted the problems she'd already done. Good! She was more than half-finished. She deserved a break. Something good to eat, maybe.

Chelsea switched on the kitchen light. She shivered a little and clutched her robe tightly around her. Now what should she have?

She snapped her fingers. Instant cocoa! She could make it in the microwave.

She heated the cocoa and carried her mug into the living room. I know, she told herself, I'll turn on the television. Only low, so Mom won't hear.

On Channel Two was an exercise program. Three women in leotards were springing up and down to the rhythm of rock music. "Uh, *one* ...uh, *two*...uh, *three*!" they shouted.

The exercises looked like fun, but it would be hard to jump while drinking cocoa.

Home shopping was on Channel Four. A lovely diamond ring cost only $29.95. "Hurry!" urged the announcer. "Call in your order before it's too late." But Chelsea didn't have $29.95.

She turned the dial. Channel Seven had news; Thirteen had news; Five had news. Channel Twenty-four had something called *Farm Report*. Hmmm...news for cows and chickens?

She turned off the TV set. Setting her empty mug on the lamp table, she picked up her math book. Let's see, she thought, eleven times five is . . . fifty-five.

Only three more to go. Two more. One more.

Chelsea stretched out her arms. "Ya-a-ay!" she said softly. Now, at last, she could get back to bed.

She turned off the lamp and got ready to switch on her pink flashlight. But she didn't need the flashlight.

Why, it must be almost morning. She had never, ever been up this late. Or was it that she had never been up this *early*?

She ran to the window. Outside it was gray and sort of misty.

The rain had stopped; puddles lay on the sidewalk and on the street. The wind had died down, too. The branches of the pine tree that stood outside the window were still.

And hanging from the tip of every pine needle was a sparkling drop of water. Diamonds! That's what they looked like.

Leaning forward, she pushed up on the window.

She raised it a few inches and reached out her hand to touch a tree branch. She held her breath. For a moment, a raindrop glistened on the end of her finger.

With her elbows on the windowsill and her chin in her cupped hands, she stayed and looked and looked.

Now the sky was turning pink, and over there, behind some trees, was a yellow glow. The sun! I never thought I'd get to see the sun rise, Chelsea said to herself.

It was the same old neighborhood, yet everything seemed different somehow—special.

A garbage truck with two men holding on in back clanked down the street. Scre-e-e-ch! The brakes squealed as the truck pulled to a stop across the road.

The men jumped down. Clang! went the metal lids onto the sidewalk. They turned the cans upside-down into the truck. Plop! went the bags of garbage.

One man, who had curly brown hair, stopped to hitch up his overalls. He glanced toward the window and saw Chelsea. She shrank back. But the man smiled and, with a wave of his hand, hopped back on the truck.

Chelsea grinned and waved back. Then she heard the r-r-ring, r-r-ring of her mother's alarm clock. And a few seconds later, her mother's voice.

"Chelsea!" called Mrs. Martin, as she did each morning. "It's time to get up!"

Chelsea giggled.

"Chelsea, are you up?"

Chelsea stretched her arms wide. "Yes, I'm up, Mom. And it's a beautiful day!"

...3...

Chelsea's Terrible Day

It was lunchtime. Chelsea was sitting in the school cafeteria, remembering the Thanksgiving play she had written a few weeks earlier.

Chelsea sighed. Mrs. Findlay had not agreed to let the class perform the play at school. "I'm afraid we don't have time," the teacher said. "We need to start practicing songs for the Christmas concert." Oh well, Mom and Dad both loved my play, thought Chelsea. Now the concert was over, and school was about to close for the winter vacation.

Mary Lynne tapped Chelsea on the arm. "I'll trade you sandwiches. How about it?"

Chelsea peered into her lunchbox. "Well...
what kind is yours?"

"Baloney."

"Oh." Chelsea did not like baloney sandwiches.
She liked peanut butter and jelly, which was what
she already had.

She wondered if Mary Lynne would be angry
if she refused to swap. If it were Katie Klein or Lucy
Burnett, Chelsea would not worry about refusing.
But Mary Lynne was her best friend, and best
friends were supposed to help each other out.

Chelsea opened her mouth to say yes, but just
then Beverly Ann started talking to Mary Lynne.

"Did you hear about the new Christmas movie,
Your Goose Is Cooked?" she asked, flipping back
her hair.

Chelsea leaned over so that she could see how
long Beverly Ann's hair was now. It rippled down
almost to her waist!

Chelsea tugged on a piece of her own brown
hair. It had taken forever to reach her shoulders.
And now it seemed stuck at that length. Maybe
it had simply decided to stop growing.

When she turned her attention back to the other girls, she discovered that Mary Lynne was already halfway through her baloney sandwich. Good! thought Chelsea. Now I won't have to trade.

Mary Lynne was in such a hurry to say something that she was talking with her mouth full. She gulped down her bite of sandwich. "I heard it's scary."

"You're crazy!" hooted Beverly Ann. "My cousin said it's babyish."

Wait a minute, thought Chelsea. I know about that movie. I've *seen* that movie. She and her mother had gone just this Saturday to celebrate Mrs. Martin's birthday.

And Mary Lynne was wrong. The movie wasn't scary. The disasters that happened were so crazy that it was funny—like the father pretending to be Santa Claus and getting stuck for a while in the chimney. And the ending was happy, after all.

Mary Lynne's forehead was wrinkled in a frown. "*My* cousin said—"

"You're wrong!" Beverly Ann interrupted.

They're both wrong, Chelsea said to herself.

The other girls didn't really know what the movie was about. They were just guessing.

She—Chelsea—was the only one at the table, maybe the only one in third grade, who had actually seen it. She had to tell them!

"Mary Lynne," Chelsea said.

Neither girl even glanced at her.

Mary Lynn glared at Beverly Ann. "Just because your cousin said so doesn't make it true!"

"My cousin doesn't lie!"

Chelsea leaned across the table and tugged at Mary Lynne's sleeve. "Mary Lynne," she said. "Mary Lynne."

Her friend turned for just a second and looked at Chelsea with a frown. It was as if she were saying, "Don't bother me, I'm busy."

Why is *she* frowning at *me*? Chelsea thought. She's the one who's hogging the conversation, as usual. Why shouldn't *I* have a chance to say something?

It was too much to put up with. She leaned forward and said in a very loud voice, "Mary Lynne!"

Silence. Everyone at the table was staring at her.

Her face felt hot. But she really wanted her friends to listen to her. And for once, she was willing to risk making Mary Lynne angry.

"I...am...trying...to...tell...you...something!"

Mary Lynne seemed puzzled. "Well, you don't have to shout."

Ooooh, she makes me so mad! thought Chelsea. "Yes, I do. I have to shout, Mary Lynne Woodlie! Because *you* talk too much. And I never get a chance to say *anything*."

She glared at Mary Lynne, and Mary Lynne stared back. Mary Lynne's big brown eyes got bigger...and bigger...and bigger!

Then she picked up her lunchbox, stood up, and walked away from the table with her nose in the air.

"Now you've done it!" declared Beverly Ann.

"Well, she does talk a lot," said Lucy Burnett.

Chelsea stared down at her lap. "I feel awful," she mumbled. She was angry with Mary Lynne and angry with herself, too, for losing her temper.

"Hey!" said a voice, and Chelsea felt a hand on her shoulder. What now? she thought, looking up. Was Mary Lynne back already?

Oh, no! *Double* oh, no! Right behind her was Billy Burnett. The way he stood there grinning made Chelsea feel like a mouse being watched by a cat.

Suddenly he reached out and snatched the hard-boiled egg she had just peeled. "Do you remember what you did to *my* lunch?" he growled.

Chelsea didn't think she could speak. She nodded her head up and down.

Lucy Burnett stuck her tongue out at her brother. "Go away, Billy. We don't want you here!"

"Okay. But first I'm gonna sque-e-eze this egg into egg salad!"

Eeeew, thought Chelsea. Billy was holding the egg right over her head! She shut her eyes.

She opened her eyes. Billy's presence at a third-grade table had attracted the attention of the cafeteria aide. She stood behind Billy and crossed her arms in a way that showed she meant business.

"Put down that young lady's egg!" she barked out. "And get back where you belong."

"Yes, Ma'am," said Billy, dropping the egg on the table. But just before he walked away, he leaned close to Chelsea and whispered, "Watch out! I'm gonna get you!"

Chelsea sighed. In just five minutes, not one, but two terrible things had happened. She'd had a fight with her best friend, and she'd been threatened again by Billy Burnett.

"You aren't going to eat that egg, are you?" said Beverly Ann. "After he's touched it?"

Chelsea shook her head. She stuck the egg back in the little plastic bag her mother had packed it in.

She decided to toss it in the trash can at the end of lunch period, but then she remembered the school rule. Kids were not supposed to throw away good food, only things like orange peels and sandwich wrappers.

She stared at the egg. It certainly wasn't *good* anymore. She didn't want to get Billy Burnett germs!

But she didn't want to get into trouble with the cafeteria aide, who was standing by the garbage cans. That would be one more terrible thing! Oh well, she would just have to carry the egg to her desk and then take it home at the end of the day.

That afternoon the class would have their holiday party. Then there would be ten days of vacation before school started again in January. What a way to start a vacation, Chelsea thought gloomily. No best friend and a fifth grader out to get me!

Lucy Burnett was tugging on her arm. "Hey, what was it you wanted to tell Mary Lynne? What was so important?"

Chelsea sighed. The movie didn't seem important at all now. "Nothing," she said sadly.

···4···

A Christmas Eve Surprise

Mrs. Martin had just taken a box of Christmas tree ornaments from a high closet shelf when the phone rang. "Why, hello, Mr. Gilbert," she said.

Oh, no! thought Chelsea. Mr. Gilbert was the supervisor of the service department at All-Star Dodge, where her mother worked. Why was he calling on her day off?

The look on her mother's face when she hung up the phone told Chelsea what was wrong. "But Mom," wailed Chelsea. "You can't go to work. It's Christmas Eve!"

"Christmas Eve is tonight. I'll be home by then."

"Well, this is Christmas Eve *day.* We were going to trim the tree!"

Her mother sighed. "I know. But the person who was supposed to work today is sick. I just have to go in; no one else can do it. We'll trim the tree this evening."

"Will we still have eggnog?" asked Chelsea. "And listen to the *Nutcracker*? Will you read 'The Night Before Christmas'?"

Mrs. Martin nodded. "We'll do it all. The eggnog is in the refrigerator; I picked it up yesterday. Hmmm, I'd better call Mrs. DeCastro and see if you can stay with her until I get home."

She patted Chelsea on the shoulder. "I know you're disappointed. But we'll have a wonderful Christmas. Don't worry."

But Chelsea did worry. Lately, her mother had seemed extra tired. When she came home from work, she changed into comfortable clothes and then sat on the sofa with her legs propped up on the coffee table. There she would stay, for half an hour at least, sipping decaf coffee and reading the newspaper.

What if she were very tired *this* evening? She might even be—horrible thought!—too tired to trim the tree.

It wouldn't be at all the kind of Christmas Eve Chelsea imagined. She wanted the tree to be all trimmed, glittering with ornaments like a princess dressed for a ball. She wanted to sit cozily beside her mother, listening to her read, while Christmas carols played in the background.

In a little while, Chelsea was sitting next door in Mrs. DeCastro's kitchen, drinking tomato soup from a mug. The baby was taking a nap, and Mrs. DeCastro was rolling cookie dough into strips with the palms of her hands.

Chelsea thought about her own house and the untrimmed Christmas tree in the living room. A plan started to shape itself in her mind. What if...what if she trimmed the tree *herself*?

What a surprise that would be for her mother! She would walk in the door, all tired out from a day at All-Star Dodge, and see a beautifully trimmed tree, ready for her to enjoy!

She swallowed the last spoonful of soup. "Mrs.

DeCastro, I need to go home! I need to do something. It's a surprise, a surprise for my mother.''

Mrs. DeCastro stopped rolling dough and looked at Chelsea. "Well, I don't know. I'm not sure what your mother would say about your being home alone for so long.''

"But you'll be right next door. I'll be okay.''

From the bedroom came the sound of the baby crying. Mrs. DeCastro looked up, distracted. "Oh, dear.'' She looked back at the half-made cookies and said, "Um...okay, Chelsea, but come and get me if you need anything.''

Chelsea hurried home. Soon she was kneeling in front of a cardboard box. It was full of decorations.

Each year a few more were added, but she could remember where almost all of them had come from. Here was a red-painted sled made from Popsicle sticks. And a reindeer made of frosted glass. Chelsea had given that to her mother when she was only six.

Thinking about her mother made her smile. She ought to be home about six, maybe even five, since it was Christmas Eve. She would walk in the door, and first thing, Chelsea would show her the tree.

"Why, Chelsea!" her mother would exclaim, her face full of amazement and delight.

Chelsea began taking things out of the box, stopping now and then to inhale the piney fragrance of the tree. Here was the tinsel they had saved from last year. She picked up the silvery strands and let them fall through her fingers. She loved tinsel!

And here were boxes of glass balls—red, gold, and green. And the tree-top star she had made in school last year. And here were the lights...oh, dear! She had forgotten about that. Last year her mother had bought strings of tiny white lights for the tree.

Chelsea wrinkled her nose slightly. The white lights were...okay.

But at the bottom of the cardboard box, she found the old set—fat, pear-shaped bulbs of red, blue, green, and yellow. Old-fashioned, her mother had said.

She sighed and reluctantly put the colored lights

back in the box. She picked up a package of white lights. Her mother had always hung the lights on the tree first. Standing on a chair to reach the top of the tree, she would arrange them just so, while Chelsea stood and watched.

But Chelsea was decorating the tree by herself this year. She decided to start with the tinsel. You can never have too much tinsel, she told herself, flinging handfuls of it at the tree.

Next came the glass balls. She had just hung the first one when the phone rang. It was her father. "How's my girl?" he said. "Did the package arrive?"

Chelsea nodded happily. Then, remembering her father couldn't see her, she said, "Yes, and I already opened it!"

"You did? Do you like it?"

Chelsea thought about the present, a cute stuffed animal. It was a life-sized yellow kitten with bright green eyes. "I love it! I named it Puff, and I'm going to keep it on my bed."

After they talked, Chelsea went slowly back to the tree. This year she was spending Christmas only with her mother. She wouldn't get to see her father at all.

Chelsea wanted to see them both. Sighing, she began to hang the rest of the balls. She missed her father very much; telephone calls and short visits just weren't the same as having him around all the time.

She knew both her parents loved her. That was the important thing. Still...she couldn't help longing for them all to be together.

She stood back to admire her work. It looked good. At least, part of it looked good. Suddenly, she realized the top of the tree was bare, while the lower branches had lots of balls.

She glanced at the clock sitting on the lamp table. Well, there wasn't time to change things around now.

Her mother could rearrange the balls later, if she wanted to. The important thing was to get most of the trimming done.

She stood back again to admire the tree; now all that was needed were the lights.

If only...if only she could use the old, colored

ones! The tree would be so much prettier. Slowly she opened the boxes that held the white lights. The strings were coiled round and round, sort of like well-behaved snakes.

Chelsea looked down at the tangle of old red, blue, green, and yellow lights that were heaped in the bottom of the big cardboard box. Then she looked back at the new white lights.

She set the new lights down. She was sure that when her mother saw how beautiful the colored lights looked on the tree, she would forget all about the white ones.

Round and round the tree she went, hopping up on a kitchen chair when she needed to loop a light over a tall branch. There! All done. She plugged them in and stood back.

Chelsea stared at the tree. Then she heard the sound of her mother, unlocking the front door.

"Oh, Mom!" Chelsea jumped up. "Stay there. Don't come in here. I have a surprise!" Quickly Chelsea unplugged the lights.

Mrs. Martin stood in the doorway, smiling. "Mrs. DeCastro told me. Is everything all right?"

"Yes, yes. Close your eyes, Mom. Don't open them until I tell you to!"

She pulled her mother into the living room. "Okay, you can open them now!"

"Oh...Chelsea," said Mrs. Martin, staring at the tree.

Chelsea looked at her mother anxiously. "Don't you like it?"

"Well, of course I like it. It was a wonderful thing to do. It's just that you used those old lights, Chelsea. Did you forget we had new ones?"

Chelsea shook her head. "I'll show you why I used the old ones. Take off your coat, Mom, and sit down."

Chelsea hung her mother's coat in the closet. "Take off your shoes, too."

Mrs. Martin laughed. "Okay."

One at a time, Chelsea picked up her mother's legs and lifted them so that her heels were resting on the coffee table. "There! Are you comfortable?"

"Yes, Chelsea, I'm comfortable."

"Okay. Just a minute." Chelsea found the

cassette tape she wanted, put it in the tape player, and turned it on. The music of *The Nutcracker Suite* filled the room.

She went to the kitchen and poured two glasses of eggnog. Carefully, she sprinkled nutmeg on top.

"Almost ready," she said, handing her mother a glass. She switched off the table lamps in the living room. With only the light from the hallway remaining, the room was almost dark. Then Chelsea plugged in the tree lights.

Chelsea curled up beside her mother on the sofa. "Look, Mom, look at the lights on the tree. Shut your eyes—but not all the way—so you can just see a little through your lashes."

Her mother sipped her eggnog. Then she narrowed her eyes. "Like this?"

"Uh-huh. Do you see, Mom?" asked Chelsea. "It's like red and blue and green rainbows, all blurry and beautiful."

Mrs. Martin looked at the lights. "Yes, Chelsea," she said softly. "You were right. It *is* beautiful."

···5···

Something Smells!

Mrs. Martin could not take time off from work during Christmas vacation. So every morning, Chelsea had to stay with Mrs. DeCastro. This was not very exciting.

Chelsea enjoyed helping with the baby, and Mrs. DeCastro tried to think of other things for her to do. But often she was a little bored and a little lonely.

Although she had really looked forward to the vacation from school, she was not having a great time. And it was all Mary Lynne's fault! It was her fault because she was still mad at Chelsea.

If only they had not had that fight! Mrs.

DeCastro would have allowed Chelsea to play at Mary Lynne's house. She lived just around the corner.

But now, everything was different. There was no visiting back and forth to see each other's gifts. There were no long afternoons spent playing together.

Of course, Chelsea did have some fun. Her mother took her to the Maryland Science Center in Baltimore on the Saturday after Christmas.

And one afternoon she went to a movie with Katie Klein. But then Katie left with her family on a skiing vacation.

Chelsea couldn't go to Lucy Burnett's house because...well, because she didn't want to run into Billy. And she couldn't ask Lucy to visit her because her mother said an extra person was too much bother for Mrs. DeCastro.

When she was lonely, she thought of her fight with Mary Lynne. Sometimes, at home after dinner, she actually picked up the telephone to call her. Then she would imagine Mary Lynne's angry voice, and she would put the phone down again.

At last it was the second of January, time to return to school. Chelsea waited on the corner, as usual, just in case Mary Lynne showed up to walk with her.

She waited and waited until it was so late she had to give up. Then she ran all the way.

When she reached the school grounds, she stopped a minute to catch her breath. To her dismay, she saw that the playground was empty. Inside the building, the classroom doors were closed. She was very late!

But when she approached the third-grade class-room, she was surprised to see all the children milling about in the hallway. And some of them were holding their noses!

Chelsea sniffed the air. Ugh! Coming from inside the classroom was a *terrible* smell!

Katie Klein saw her and came over. "Isn't it awful?" she said, grinning.

Chelsea nodded. "What happened?"

Katie shrugged. "Nobody knows for sure. Mrs. Findlay thinks an animal got trapped in the building over vacation and died."

Chelsea was horrified. A dead animal in the third-grade classroom! If it was true, she was sure she would never be able to do a speck of work in there again.

Peeking in the open door, she saw Mrs. Findlay standing in the middle of the room. As usual, the teacher was dressed beautifully, in high heels and a silky dress.

She held a lace-edged handkerchief over her nose.

The gray-haired school custodian, Mr. Banks, muttered to himself as he paced around the room. Every once in a while he would stop suddenly and lift up the lid of a desk. After rummaging around in it a bit, he would shake his head and continue pacing.

Without knowing quite why, Chelsea felt a little prickle at the back of her neck. It was a feeling that she'd done something wrong but didn't know—or couldn't remember—what it was.

Then Chelsea heard Mr. Banks say, "Something rotten," and "Spoiled food, that's what it smells like to me."

Chelsea felt more uncomfortable. But how, she asked herself, could she have anything to do with the awful smell?

Uh-oh! Now Mr. Banks was standing over *her* desk. Now he was opening it.

He removed Chelsea's books. Then. . ."Aha!" he cried. He pulled out a little plastic bag.

"Here's the culprit, Ma'am. This. . ." He stared at the bag. "Whatever it is. The books smashed it against the back of the desk, and it just turned plain rotten!"

He carried the plastic bag over to show the teacher. He dangled it in front of her face, and Mrs. Findlay backed up.

Her dainty hands flew to cover her nose, making her gold bracelets jingle. "Take it away," she begged. "And, thank you, Mr. Banks."

Buzzing with questions, the third graders crowded around the doorway. Only Chelsea stood like a statue.

That gooey, slimy mess in the plastic bag was *her egg*! Her hard-boiled egg that she'd forgotten to take home. Left here throughout the holiday, it had grown moldy and smelly.

"You won't be able to use your desk for a while, Chelsea," said Mrs. Findlay. "Not till we get it cleaned up."

Now Mr. Banks was back. He and the teacher lifted Chelsea's desk and carried it out the side door.

Chelsea looked down at the floor. Everyone was staring at her! Why, oh why, did this have to happen? Would Mrs. Findlay yell?

As it turned out, she simply said, "Class, let this be a lesson to you. *Please* do not leave any food items at school."

She took some books off an extra desk at the back of the room and pulled it to Chelsea's row. "You can use this for now."

Chelsea felt like running from the room or even—crying! She took a deep, trembling breath and managed to store her things in the new desk.

The class was settling down. Mrs. Findlay was writing the spelling work on the blackboard. Maybe, thought Chelsea, if she behaved *very* well the rest of the day, everyone would forget she had anything to do with the terrible, rotten odor.

Once, she looked up from her work and caught Mary Lynne staring at her. With all the fuss about the egg, she had almost forgotten about the fight with her best friend.

Chelsea gave her a shy little smile. But instead of smiling back, Mary Lynne looked down and quickly started writing on her spelling paper.

My used-to-be best friend, Chelsea reminded herself sadly.

When recess began, she zipped up her coat and ran outside with the rest of the class. Her friends were taking turns on the tire swing. "I'm after you!" she called out, taking a place behind Beverly Ann.

Beverly Ann turned around and stared at Chelsea coldly. "You're the one who made that awful smell!"

Now they were all staring at her!

"I didn't mean to," said Chelsea. She would never have done such a thing on purpose—didn't Beverly Ann know that?

"I just forgot—"

Beverly Ann interrupted. "Well, I think it was a babyish thing to do."

Chelsea felt her cheeks turn red. She couldn't let Beverly Ann get away with that! She had to say something to show how grown up she really was. "I am *not* a baby! And I'm going to...to get my ears pierced, so there!"

At these words, Chelsea's used-to-be best friend, Mary Lynne, let out a gasp. Too late, Chelsea remembered that Mary Lynne knew all about Mrs. Martin's views on ear piercing.

"Really?" asked Katie Klein. "I'm not allowed."

"Me, neither," said Lucy Burnett. "Not till next year. Anyway, doesn't it hurt?"

"Of course it doesn't," said Beverly Ann, touching her earlobe. Her ears were already pierced.

"Well..." Chelsea hesitated. Perhaps she had better back out of this before it was too late.

Then Beverly Ann whispered something to Mary Lynne. Mary Lynne covered her mouth with her hand and giggled.

Chelsea's heart was filled with sadness. Her best friend was laughing at her. Her used-to-be best friend.

Beverly Ann tossed her head. "I think you're lying. I don't think you're going to get your ears pierced at all!"

"I am, too!" replied Chelsea, recklessly. "Tonight!"

···6···

An Ear-Piercing Problem

Chelsea woke up with a sense of doom hanging over her. Last night she had tried with all her might to change her mother's mind about pierced ears.

"Please, please, please," she had begged.

Her mother sighed. "I already told you, Chelsea. You're not old enough."

Chelsea pouted. "It's not fair! *You* have earrings. Why can't I?"

"I didn't get my ears pierced till I was eighteen. You'll just have to wait awhile, and that's *final*."

Now Chelsea ran to the window, hoping to see drifts of fresh snow. A blizzard would be wonderful. It would close the schools.

But there had not been a storm. The same old white stuff, dirty and gray now, covered the ground in thin patches. Chelsea climbed sadly back into bed.

It was time to put Emergency Plan A into action.

"Mo-om," she croaked. "I don't feel good."

Her mother came in. "Hmmm." Mrs. Martin laid her hand on Chelsea's forehead. "You don't feel hot, but we'll check your temperature to make sure."

With the thermometer in her mouth, Chelsea tried to think warm thoughts. Bonfires...chili with peppers...her new wool sweater.

No luck.

"Your temperature's normal, Chelsea. Let me see your throat."

"Aaaah." Chelsea stretched her mouth open.

"It's not red," said her mother briskly. "Get dressed, and we'll see how you feel after breakfast."

Chelsea sighed. Plan A did not seem to be working. On to Plan B. Plan B was not very good, but right now it was the only one she had.

When it was almost time to leave for school and work, her mother stopped buttoning her coat and looked at Chelsea. "Honey, you seem unhappy. I hope you're not still upset about the earrings. Or—is anything else wrong?"

Chelsea shook her head. There was nothing her mother could do now. Even if she changed her mind, Chelsea knew it was too late to get her ears pierced before school. She would just have to handle the problem another way.

When she reached the end of the walk that led from the front door, she stopped and looked back. Good! Her mother was no longer watching from the window. Chelsea pulled a pair of bright red earmuffs from her coat pocket and jammed them on her head.

The earmuffs belonged to Mrs. Martin, and they matched her new coat. I hope Mom doesn't mind my borrowing them, thought Chelsea. After all, it's an emergency.

As soon as she got them adjusted over her ears, the earmuffs began to slip. Slowly, slowly

they crept toward the back of her head. Then—
bo-o-oing—they popped off.

Ooooh, thought Chelsea, as she picked them up. I hate earmuffs! But she *had* to wear them. They covered up her ears.

She bent forward a little, so that she was looking at her toes. Maybe if she walked like this, the earmuffs wouldn't slide backwards.

A thin layer of week-old packed snow covered the sidewalk. Crunch, crunch went her pink-and-white boots. She couldn't see where she was going, but as long as she stayed on the path, she'd be all right.

When she reached the curb at the corner, she looked up. And there was her used-to-be best friend, Mary Lynne Woodlie, standing beside her.

"It won't work," said Mary Lynne flatly, without even saying hello.

She meant the earmuffs, of course. But Chelsea was more interested in the fact that Mary Lynne was waiting for her. She was filled with hope. Maybe. . .maybe Mary Lynne wanted to be friends again.

"I thought you were mad at me," Chelsea said aloud.

"Well . . . ," Mary Lynne seemed embarrassed. "I *was*. But Beverly Ann came over to my house yesterday after school, and it was no fun at all!"

"Really?" Chelsea smiled.

"Yes, and anyway, you were mad at me, too."

Chelsea didn't say anything at first. But she had to admit to herself that it was true. For a while at least, she *had* been angry.

But being without a best friend was terrible! She wanted very much to make up with Mary Lynne.

"I didn't mean to hurt your feelings. I shouldn't have said you talk too much."

The two girls turned toward school. "That's okay," said Mary Lynne. "I guess I do talk too much."

She snapped her fingers. "I know what! Today I'm going to listen, and you do the talking."

"Oh, good," said Chelsea, happily. The rest of the day might be awful; she would have to face Beverly Ann. But, in spite of that, it was wonderful to have a best friend once more. She would never get angry at Mary Lynne again; she was sure of it.

Mary Lynne tapped her on the shoulder. "Well, aren't you going to say something?"

Oh, yes, that's right, thought Chelsea. This was her chance. She was supposed to be doing the talking. The trouble was, she wasn't used to chattering the way Mary Lynne did. She was used to listening and thinking her own thoughts.

"Um...what shall we talk about?"

"How about those?" said Mary Lynne, pointing to the earmuffs.

Chelsea was holding on to them with one hand while she walked. "What about them? I just have cold ears today. That's all."

Mary Lynne shook her head. "I know you didn't get your ears pierced. And Beverly Ann will know it right away, too. If you had earrings, you would want to show them off—not cover them up!"

"Nobody will know for sure," said Chelsea, stubbornly. "Not if I keep the earmuffs on all day."

"You can't keep them on all day!"

"Yes, I can!"

Mary Lynne shrugged and, forgetting her promise not to talk, began to tell Chelsea all about a new game she'd gotten for Christmas.

Chelsea hadn't forgotten. But she had just discovered something; she enjoyed it when Mary Lynne did most of the talking. That's one of the reasons we're best friends, she thought. She's a good talker, and I'm a good listener.

The two girls waited until the last minute to duck into the classroom. As Chelsea slid into her seat, Beverly Ann gave her a surprised look. She stared at the earmuffs.

She doesn't know *for sure*, Chelsea told herself.

In the middle of math period, Mrs. Findlay noticed the earmuffs. "Chelsea," said the teacher in a puzzled voice, "Are your ears cold, dear?"

Chelsea gave her head a shake, then hastily grabbed at the earmuffs to keep them from falling off. "No...I mean, yes. I just want to wear earmuffs today, Mrs. Findlay."

"What will they think of next?" said her

teacher. "All right. If you want to wear earmuffs, it's fine with me."

Mary Lynne stood beside Chelsea at the pencil sharpener. "What are you going to do about recess?" she whispered. "What if Beverly Ann grabs them off?"

Chelsea glanced across the room. Oh dear, Beverly Ann was staring at her! She was whispering something to Katie Klein. "I'll. . . I'll stay inside during recess. I'll read a book," Chelsea said.

"But what about tomorrow? You're not going to wear those earmuffs again, are you?"

Chelsea shrugged. She had been trying not to think about *that*.

...7...

Cat Eyes

Mrs. Martin kept her sewing basket in her bedroom closet. Before dinner, Chelsea tiptoed into the room and rummaged through the basket till she found a packet of needles.

Then, looking over her shoulder, she scuttled into the bathroom. She locked the door.

She pulled a small wooden stool in front of the sink and stepped up on it. She could see herself in the mirror, but she wanted to get a little closer.

She climbed from the stepstool onto the sink. She perched on the edge of it, with her feet in the basin, and stared at her reflection.

There's nothing to worry about, she said to

her frightened-looking face. People get their ears pierced all the time.

With her left hand, she pushed back her hair and held her earlobe. With her right hand, she took a firm grip on the needle.

Was it sharp enough? Chelsea let go of her earlobe and touched the pointed end. "Ouch!" It *was* sharp—very, very sharp.

Maybe, she thought, if I sort of shut my eyes, I can concentrate on my ear, not the needle. Then it will be over before I know it.

Chelsea squinted into the mirror. Slowly she brought her right hand toward her ear.

She suddenly remembered a television commercial advertising the movie to be shown on Channel Five that evening—*Jaws*.

As far as Chelsea could tell, the movie was about a big shark that went after people. A big shark with needle-sharp teeth.

Her right hand was coming closer; the great white shark was circling its victim—coming closer . . .and closer.

She could almost hear the eerie *Jaws* music

from the commercial. *Da*-da! *Da*-da! *Da*-da!

The needle touched her earlobe. Prick! The great white shark was attacking! Chelsea squeezed her eyes shut and pushed!

"O-o-ow!" That *hurt*!

Her mother called from the living room. "Chelsea! What happened?"

Chelsea opened her eyes. "Nothing!"

Had the needle gone all the way through? It must have, to hurt that much. She pulled back her hair and stared in the mirror. There was a tiny red mark on the lobe of her ear. That was all.

She stared at the needle in disbelief. Something had gone wrong. She decided to put it back in her mother's sewing basket.

After dinner, Mrs. Martin went next door to see Mrs. DeCastro. Chelsea called Mary Lynne.

"You didn't do it right," said Mary Lynne. "You're supposed to hold an ice cube on your ear first."

"Ice?" Chelsea didn't like the sound of that. "For how long?"

"Till your ear is so numb it doesn't hurt when

you pinch it. About half an hour, I guess."

"Oh." Chelsea thought about ice and how it would feel pressed against her bare skin. And what would her mother say when she noticed the holes?

"Chelsea...Chelsea, are you still there?"

"Yes," answered Chelsea. "But Mary Lynne, I think I'll have to try something else."

. . .

At school the next morning, Chelsea pulled Mary Lynne into the girls' rest room. "Come on, we've got five minutes till the bell rings."

Chelsea took a folded tissue from her pocket. "Look," she said, unwrapping it. "I'm going to glue these on my ears to look like earrings."

Mary Lynne leaned closer. She stared at the shiny, green objects in Chelsea's palm. "What are those?"

"Well, they're really Puff's eyes. You know, my stuffed kitten?"

Mary Lynne seemed surprised. "The one you got for Christmas? The one you keep on your bed?"

Chelsea felt uncomfortable. "It's just for a little

while. I'll glue them back on Puff later, when Beverly Ann forgets all about pierced ears.''

Mary Lynne frowned. ''What makes you think she's going to forget—*ever*?''

''Well, she might,'' said Chelsea unhappily. ''Anyway, look. I found this glue at home.'' Out of her backpack she took a dented plastic tube. ''I can use it to stick them on.''

Mary Lynne wrinkled her forehead. ''It's not the type of glue that works real fast and never comes off, is it?''

Chelsea shook her head. ''My mother won't buy that kind. Not since she heard about a little boy who glued his finger to his nose.''

''Okay then,'' said Mary Lynne. ''We'd better hurry.''

While Chelsea held her hair out of the way, Mary Lynne dabbed a bit of glue on each of Chelsea's ears. ''Hold still,'' said Mary Lynne. She pressed the cat eyes onto the sticky spots.

''Wait a minute!'' Mary Lynne said suddenly. ''What are you going to do about your mother?''

''Oh, I've already thought of that. I'll just take

the earrings off before she gets home.''

''How? What if they don't *come* off, once the glue dries?''

''I don't know.'' Chelsea frowned, but then decided she couldn't worry about that now. She checked herself in the mirror. ''Oh, good! They look real, don't they?''

Mary Lynne nodded and grabbed Chelsea's arm.

''Come on, let's go!''

They got to their classroom just as the bell rang. I'll show *her*, Chelsea thought, as she passed Beverly Ann's desk. She reached up and hooked her hair behind her ears, to show off her ''earrings.''

Katie Klein nudged Beverly Ann, then whispered something to her. As Chelsea took her seat, she could feel Beverly Ann's eyes on her. She glanced over her shoulder.

Beverly Ann's mouth curved down. Her eyebrows looked like one straight line. Chelsea smiled sweetly at her before turning back to the front. Humming a little tune under her breath, she got out her spelling book.

After dinner, Mary Lynne called. "Did you get the earrings off all right? Or did your mom catch you with them on?"

Chelsea glanced sideways at her mother. "Yes," she whispered, "and no." She picked up the telephone and walked around the corner, as far as the cord could reach.

"I just pulled them off," she whispered. "That was easy. But I had to pick off the glue."

"But it all came off? Great!"

"Uh-huh," said Chelsea. As she spoke, she touched her left ear. She didn't tell Mary Lynne that her ears were a bit red and felt funny. Sort of itchy.

Again the next morning, Chelsea took the green plastic cat eyes to school. Mary Lynne guarded the door of the rest room while Chelsea dabbed blobs of glue on her ears.

Three days later the plan was still working. Mary Lynne congratulated Chelsea during recess. "I can't believe how well it's going! Nobody knows they're not real."

"Yeah, I guess so." Chelsea glanced at Beverly Ann, twirling around on the tire swing. Almost all the third-grade girls had complimented her on her new earrings. Beverly Ann had not said a word.

"Old Miss Smarty-Pants just doesn't want to admit she was wrong!" snorted Mary Lynne.

Chelsea grinned. Then she thought of something, and her smile disappeared. "How long do you think I'll have to keep this up? Sticking the earrings on every morning, I mean."

Mary Lynne shrugged. "I don't know. Till June, I suppose...till school ends."

Chelsea patted her ear. She felt a twinge of pain and winced. Now her ears were definitely sore, especially the left one.

And there were tiny bumps, like blisters, all over her earlobes. It's lucky I have hair long enough to cover my ears, Chelsea thought. Otherwise Mom would notice. And that would spoil the whole plan.

Later that day, Chelsea sat quietly listening to Katie Klein read aloud. She followed closely in her book; it was her turn next.

Mrs. Findlay nodded. "All right, Chelsea."

"It was a very hot day—"Chelsea began.

Suddenly, from across the circle of chairs, Mary Lynne interrupted. "Chelsea, your left ear! It's as big as a grapefruit!"

Faces turned toward her, mouths dropped open, and Chelsea felt her cheeks get hot.

"Chelsea," said the teacher, "you'd better see the nurse."

In the nurse's office, Chelsea's reflection stared back at her from the shiny surface of a paper-towel dispenser. It wasn't true what Mary Lynne had said. Her earlobe was not as big as a grapefruit. A plum, maybe, or a plump cherry. But not a grapefruit.

"Well, this *is* a sight," said the school nurse briskly. "Your ear is swollen up all around your earring."

She washed her hands at the sink. "First, we've got to unfasten those things."

Chelsea squirmed. Uh-oh, she thought.

"You can't unfasten them," she whispered.

"Don't worry," said the nurse kindly. "I'll be very gentle."

Chelsea shook her head. "No. I mean, they're not real earrings." She explained about the glue.

"I see," said the nurse slowly. "In that case. . ."

She went to a cupboard and took out a bottle of something. "This will just take a minute. Then you'll be good as new."

Hmmm, thought Chelsea, as an idea struck her. "Can you put bandages on my ears, please?"

The nurse raised her eyebrows. "Well, sure. If it'll make you feel better."

She got some supplies from the cupboard. "You know, I think you must be allergic to that glue."

Oh, thought Chelsea. That explains it!

Soon she was on her way back to the classroom. She fingered Puff's green eyes in her pocket, then put up both hands to touch her bandaged ears.

"Tsk, tsk," said Mrs. Findlay. "It's a shame, but sometimes that happens with pierced ears." She shook her head, causing her own dangly earrings to sway from side to side.

Chelsea nodded. She could see Mary Lynne giggling with her hand over her mouth.

Katie Klein raised her hand and told about a

friend whose pierced ears had become infected. "And green gooey stuff came pouring out—"

"Thank you, Katie," said Mrs. Findlay hastily. "And now, class, let's get back to work."

Beverly Ann waited for Chelsea and Mary Lynne after school. "I bet you forgot to clean your ears," she said, tossing back her long hair. "When I got mine done, I wiped them three times a day with alcohol."

Ooooh, thought Chelsea, I wish you would just keep quiet.

But Beverly Ann went on. "The holes are going to close up now, I bet. You probably wish *you* had taken better care of—"

Chelsea surprised herself by interrupting. "I don't *want* to wear earrings now. It's...it's too much trouble, that's what. So there!"

Beverly Ann stared at her. Mary Lynne grinned and held up her thumb in a victory sign.

But Chelsea didn't notice. She was imagining herself wearing a pair of shiny little golden hoops. Someday, she thought, someday when I'm older, I *will* get my ears pierced!

···8···

Yummy or Yucky?

"**W**hat do you mean you don't want to go to Lucy's party?" exclaimed Mary Lynne. It was Saturday afternoon, and she had just arrived at Chelsea's house. "You *have* to go!"

"Shhh! Not so loud." Chelsea pulled Mary Lynne into her bedroom and closed the door. "I told my mother I have a stomachache."

"Okay," whispered Mary Lynne. "I'll talk softer."

She plopped down on Chelsea's pink bedspread. "But I still say you have to go! All the girls in our class are going."

She paused to take a breath and then rattled

on. "They're going to have a real magician. Lucy said so! And he's going to make those balloon animals, you know? And Lucy's going to give out really good prizes for games! And that's not all— they're having hot-fudge sundaes!"

Chelsea sighed. She didn't want to hear how great the party was going to be.

Mary Lynne jumped up. "Just tell me—give me one good reason. *Why* can't you go?"

"I've already told you. I can't go because of Billy. If he's at the party, he'll get me!"

"Lucy's brother?" Mary Lynne raised her eyebrows. "I can't believe you're still afraid of him! I'll bet he's forgotten all about what you did to his lunch. That was ages ago—way back in the fall!"

Chelsea sighed again. She picked up her doll, Susan, and began fiddling with her dress. Mary Lynne didn't understand. She thought just because Billy hadn't done anything yet, it meant he wasn't *going* to do anything. But Chelsea knew better.

Oh sure, for a while it seemed that he had

forgotten about his smashed lunch. Or more likely, just decided that she, Chelsea, wasn't worth bothering about. But then, last Monday, things changed.

Chelsea was line leader that day. Going down the hallway, she turned and walked backwards a few steps to make sure everyone was following her.

She wasn't watching where she was going. And *bang*!—she bumped right into someone coming from the other direction.

She heard a yelp. "Ow!" She whirled around and came face-to-face with—Billy Burnett!

"Ow! Ow! Ow! That hurt!" Billy hopped up and down, clutching his foot.

"Oh! Sorry." Chelsea stood still, looking at him uneasily, while the other third-graders moved off down the hallway.

"Yeah, I'll bet!" He stuck out his tongue. "You'd better watch out, Chelsea Martin!"

Chelsea stared as he limped off. Then she hurried to catch up with her line. Well, I *am* sorry, she told herself. I didn't mean to step on him. He's making an awfully big fuss!

Later, she wondered if tramping on his foot had reminded him of that time months ago when she had tramped on his banana. Now he was probably angry with her all over again.

On Friday, as she was leaving school with Mary Lynne, she had another run-in with Billy. He passed her going out the big front doors of the building.

Jerking to a stop, he called, "Wait a minute!" to his friends.

He ran back and stood, like a wall, right in front of her. "I'll see you at the party tomorrow, Chelsea!" Raising one eyebrow, he grinned evilly. "Heh, heh, heh!"

Now, remembering the look on his face, Chelsea felt a little shivery. Billy must be planning some *horrible* revenge.

Maybe he would tie her to a tree. Or lock her in a dark closet.

In any case, it was sure to be something she didn't like. And that's why she could not, absolutely *not,* go to Lucy's party.

"Chelsea, are you listening?" Mary Lynne

said. "I bet he won't even be there!"

"Yes, he will," insisted Chelsea. "You heard him yesterday."

"Oh...that. He was just teasing."

Chelsea shook her head. "I don't think so."

"We-ell." Mary Lynne twisted a strand of her black hair around her finger. "I think you're getting all upset about nothing. Okay—how about this? We'll go to Lucy's house and peek in the window. If we don't see Billy, we'll go inside."

"What if we *do* see him?"

"If we see him, you can go home again. He'll never even know you were there."

Chelsea hesitated. If she returned home early, how could she explain it to her mother?

"I'll leave, too, if he's there," said Mary Lynne. "We'll go to my house and play Monopoly."

"Really?" Mary Lynne was a great best friend! Chelsea thought about the plan for a minute. "Well, okay, I'll go."

Mary Lynne grinned. "All right!"

"Wait a minute!" said Chelsea, frowning. "I

told my mother I had a stomachache!''

Mary Lynne shrugged. ''Just say that you're feeling better now.''

''Okay.'' The girls found Mrs. Martin in the kitchen, and Chelsea explained that her stomach-ache had disappeared.

They went to find their boots and coats and their gifts. Mary Lynne had brought an Operation game, and Chelsea had picked out a one-year diary with a key.

Lucy's house was four blocks away, close enough to walk. Chelsea clumped along, kicking at the melting snow at the edge of the sidewalk.

Mary Lynne chattered away about the party. ''This is going to be so much fun! I've never seen a real magician. Not in person, I mean. Have you? I wonder if he'll make somebody disappear.''

She stooped to pick up a handful of slush. She formed it into a ball and tossed it up in the air.

Chelsea watched it go splat! on the sidewalk in front of them. All at once, she pictured Billy Burnett tossing *her* into the air like a snowball.

She could almost see herself flying through

space, arms and legs sticking out every which way. And then landing splat! on the sidewalk.

Anxiously, she turned to Mary Lynne. "Remember—we're going to peek through the window before we go in. If he's there, we're leaving. Right?"

"Okay, okay. We already decided that."

In five minutes, they turned the corner onto Lucy's street. "Look!" Chelsea pointed. "There's Katie. Her parents just dropped her off."

"Come on!" Mary Lynne broke into a trot.

Chelsea hurried to keep up. Then, as they got to the front walk of Lucy's house, Chelsea slowed down. But Mary Lynne headed straight down the cleared path to the door.

"Hey!" cried Chelsea. "Wait a minute! We have to check first to see if Billy's here."

Mary Lynne stopped in front of the porch steps. She frowned. "Oh, all right."

She pointed to the side of the house. "How about that window?"

"Okay." Chelsea stepped carefully through the melting snow. She squeezed through some low evergreens. Now she was close enough to peer inside.

"Can you see anything?" asked Mary Lynne.

"No. Here, hold this a minute." Chelsea handed her present to Mary Lynne.

She put her mittened hands on the window sill and leaned forward. Her nose pressed against the pane. It was cold!

Her breath made a white spot on the glass. She wiped it away with her mitten.

"Now I see Katie, taking off her coat. And Mrs. Burnett...and that's all."

"Okay. Billy's not there." Mary Lynne stamped up and down. "Come on, let's go in. I got some snow in my boots, and my feet are freezing!"

"But maybe he's in another part of the house. I think we should wait awhile and—"

"What on earth are you two *doing*?" said a voice. It was Beverly Ann. Her hands on her hips, she was watching them from the sidewalk.

Mary Lynne shrugged. "Nothing!" She glanced at Chelsea. "We were just about to go inside, right?"

Unhappily, Chelsea nodded. I can't tell Beverly Ann about Billy, she thought. She'd call me chicken! And I can't leave now, either. Not with *her* watching.

Chelsea and Mary Lynne made their way through the slippery snow to the porch. Beverly Ann jabbed at the doorbell with her index finger.

"Oh, good. Here you are," said Mrs. Burnett as she opened the door. "You three are the last to arrive."

As Chelsea unzipped her pink parka and removed her boots, she quickly looked around. No sign of Billy. Good!

Mrs. Burnett led the way into the living room. It was decorated for the party in purple, Lucy's favorite color. Purple streamers criss-crossed the room. And a huge bunch of purple and white balloons dangled from the ceiling.

Giggling third-graders crowded together on the sofa and chairs. Lucy, looking very excited, waved and smiled at them.

"Sit here, girls," said Mrs. Burnett. Mr. Burnett set out three folding chairs.

Lucy's mother walked to the center of the room. "I think we're ready to begin."

She signaled to someone in the hallway. And a tall man, made taller by his pointed hat, walked quickly into the room.

He had very dark skin and very white teeth, and he wore a long coat spangled with stars. Over one arm he carried something made of brown, furry cloth.

In a deep voice he said, "Good afternoon, Ladies! I am the Great Magnifico!"

Then Chelsea heard a high, squeaky voice. "Hello!" She looked around. Who was talking?

"I am the Great Oswald!"

Chelsea stared. The voice was coming from the brown, furry thing—a monkey! But that couldn't be. Then Chelsea realized what was happening—the Great Magnifico was a ventriloquist!

The monkey and the magician talked back and forth and joked with the audience. Whenever the monkey spoke, Chelsea watched the magician carefully. But she could never catch him moving his mouth!

After a while, the Great Magnifico put the monkey away. He got out a deck of cards and did some tricks. Then he pulled a quarter out of Mrs. Burnett's ear. While she sat there looking surprised, he took a silk handkerchief from her other ear.

Mary Lynne covered her mouth with her hand and giggled. Chelsea laughed out loud when he pulled a bouquet of roses from Katie Klein's mouth.

The Magician took a long skinny balloon out of his pocket. He stretched it once or twice and gave it a few twists. And there was a long-eared balloon dog.

He handed it to Lucy. "Who's next?" he asked.

"Me...me, me!" cried the girls. Soon they all had a balloon animal to take home. At the end of the performance, the Great Magnifico gave a deep bow. Everyone clapped and cheered.

"All right now," said Mrs. Burnett when the clapping died down. "It's time for ice cream and cake. Then we'll have games, and Lucy will open the presents."

Holding her balloon giraffe, Chelsea stood up and stretched. Then suddenly, she heard a voice behind her.

"Well, well, well. Look who's here."

It was Lucy's brother! He *was* at the party.

Just then Mrs. Burnett called from the kitchen. "Billy! Come here and help, please!"

"Coming, Mom!" Billy pointed his index finger like a pistol at Chelsea. "Catch *you* later!"

Oo-o-oh! Chelsea's stomach felt strange. She sank back down on the folding chair.

Mary Lynne came up to her. "Come on, let's go get some ice cream."

Before Chelsea could answer, Mrs. Burnett bustled into the room. "Girls! Please come along now. We're going to sing 'Happy Birthday.'"

Along with the rest of the straggling guests, Chelsea was herded into the kitchen. The chairs at the dinette set were already taken, but there was a folding table with a few places left.

"Let's sit here," said Mary Lynne. She and Chelsea squeezed in across from Katie and Beverly Ann.

Chelsea whispered into Mary Lynne's ear. "Billy's here! Did you see him?"

"Don't worry," Mary Lynne whispered back. "He won't do anything to you in front of his parents."

"Oh...that's right." Chelsea began to feel a little more comfortable.

Across the table, Katie Klein smiled at her. She was dropping M&Ms into her mouth, one by one.

Chelsea picked up a handful of candy, too, and began to divide it up according to color. Dark brown here, light brown here, red over there...

Suddenly Mary Lynne jabbed her elbow into Chelsea's ribs. Chelsea looked up. Billy was standing there, right behind her chair!

His cheeks were pink. His eyes danced. And the expression on his face said clearly, "I'll get you now, Chelsea Martin!"

But how? She looked around to make sure his parents were still in the room.

Yes, Mr. Burnett was pouring drinks. And Mrs. Burnett was serving each of the girls at the dinette table an ice cream sundae.

He won't try anything with his parents standing right there, thought Chelsea. He's just trying to scare me. She tossed her head. Well, maybe—maybe I won't let him!

"Hey, Chelsea! Got something for you!" Billy set an ice cream sundae down on the table in front of her.

Mmmm, it looked scrumptious. Chocolate-fudge sauce oozed over vanilla ice cream. And to top it off, whipped cream and a cherry.

Chelsea picked up her spoon and stuck it into the creamy topping. She lifted the spoon to her mouth. Then she stopped.

Coming from behind her—from Billy—was a little sound. A sound like a giggle.

She stuck the spoon back in the dish and looked around at her friends. Nobody else at this table had her ice cream yet.

All at once, Chelsea *knew*. Billy had done something to the sundae. And his parents were so busy, they hadn't even noticed!

Maybe he used shaving cream instead of whipping cream? Or maybe that stuff her mother put on her hair. Mousse, that was it.

Billy leaned over the table. "Come on," he said impatiently. "Come on! Take a bite!"

Chelsea wondered what to do. If she did stick a spoonful in her mouth—who knows?—it might poison her!

She pictured herself clutching her throat. "Arrrgh!" Then she would tumble off the chair and onto the kitchen floor. *Crash*!

But if she refused to take a bite, wouldn't he just think of some other way to get even?

Then she had an idea. Slowly she raised the dish so that it was close to her mouth.

She stuck out her tongue and just touched the tip of it to the creamy topping. Oh! Ugh! Whatever it was, it tasted terrible!

Billy sputtered with laughter. "You should see the look on your face!"

"You got me, Billy. Now take it away. Please!" Chelsea handed him the sundae.

"Okay." Billy smiled. "At least you weren't afraid to try it." He turned the dish upside down in the sink.

A few minutes later, all the girls at the folding table were served. "This one's real," said Billy, handing Chelsea another dish of ice cream.

She looked at it doubtfully.

"Go ahead," said Billy. "You can trust me. And you know something? You're a pretty good sport, Chelsea Martin!"

...9...

Valentine's Day

"**D**o you know what day it is?" asked Chelsea at dinner one evening.

Her mother nodded. "February second—Groundhog Day."

"Yes! In art class we drew pictures of a groundhog peeping out of his hole. But. . ." Chelsea made a face, "the teacher told us he saw his shadow, so that means six more weeks of winter."

Mrs. Martin smiled. "Cheer up. It also means Valentine's Day will be here in twelve days."

"That's right!"

After dinner Chelsea sat with her chin in her hand, daydreaming. She tried to picture what Valentine's Day would be like in third grade.

In second grade, the teacher had brought a large cardboard box into class. Everyone helped to decorate it with red construction paper and white cut-out hearts. A slot was cut in the top for the valentines.

Just thinking about the box made Chelsea eager to get started on her cards.

"You'll have to wait," said her mother. "We haven't even bought them yet."

"But, Mom, I think I had some left over last year."

In the back of her closet, under a pile of games, Chelsea found a shoebox. It contained a list of students from second grade, a number of unused cards, and all the valentines she'd received last year.

"Oh, here's a funny one." She picked up a Dennis-the-Menace card. "From Bobby." A card with a cute kitten was signed, "Love, Mary Lynne." Chelsea decided to read them all.

"Let's see, that's one...two..." She counted eighteen cards.

She stared at the valentines in her hand, struck by a sudden, unpleasant thought. There had been twenty-four people in her second-grade classroom. Somehow, she had never noticed something—six people had not sent her cards!

But who? She got out the list of names to match against the signatures on the valentines. Ah-hah! No card from Dennis. Chelsea drew a frowning Mr. Yuk face beside his name.

Her mother poked her head in the doorway. "Chelsea, do you have enough cards?"

Chelsea counted the unused valentines. "Yes. I guess we bought extra."

"That's right. I remember thinking it would save a trip this year. Okay, if your homework's done, you can get started on them."

. . .

"Are these your valentines?" asked Chelsea's mother later. She picked up a small bundle of white envelopes held by a rubber band and flipped through it.

"Did you check the list Mrs. Findlay sent home?"

Chelsea looked up from her book.

"Chelsea!" said her mother. "You only have sixteen cards here."

"I know. I'm not giving them to the boys, Mom."

"But didn't the instructions from Mrs. Findlay say...look, here they are."

In capital letters, at the bottom of the paper, were the words PLEASE GIVE A VALENTINE TO EVERYONE ON THE LIST.

"Oh, Mom! Do I have to? Even the boys?"

"Yes," said her mother firmly.

Chelsea grumbled to herself. This wasn't fair at all. Aloud, she said, "Last year, some of the boys didn't give me one."

"That's why Mrs. Findlay has that rule, so this year no one will have hurt feelings."

Chelsea sighed. Then she got out the rest of the unused valentines and sat down with them in front of the television.

At least she didn't have to send the boys *nice* cards, she thought, searching for ones with silly riddles or jokes. It was a waste of time to send some dumb old boy a lovely valentine when she didn't even like him, anyhow.

"Are *you* looking for a card for that certain someone?"

Startled, Chelsea looked up. Oh, it was just a television commercial.

She dropped the valentines and watched the screen. A beautiful young woman was reading a greeting card, a handsome young man standing by her side. Chelsea was fascinated by the dreamy expression on the woman's face.

Now the young woman looked up at the handsome man. They looked deep, deep, deep into each other's eyes. "Make your Valentine's Day special," crooned the announcer.

Ooooh! Chelsea was filled with delight. A wonderful idea popped into her head. Wouldn't it be fun—wouldn't it be exciting—if she sent a romantic card to somebody? To a *boy*!

She snatched up the list of third graders. Hmmm, who should it be? John? No. Timothy? No, definitely not.

And not Gregory, who sat behind her. She

suspected him of snitching her pencils. She ran her finger down the list of names. No! nope! ...well, maybe.

Here was someone who wasn't *too* bad— Arthur Wilmot. He was the tallest boy in third grade. Some girls even thought he looked like a fifth-grader!

Chelsea half-closed her eyes, like the girl on television. Arthur, she murmured. Oh, Arthur! Da-a-ahling!

She would make a card for him. A beautiful card!

Carefully, she cut red paper into the shape of a big heart. There! That looked good, but it was too plain.

"Mom!" she called. "Do you have any lace?"

Mrs. Martin came into the kitchen, where Chelsea was working. "Oh, you want something to trim that heart? But I thought you finished your valentines."

"I did, and I made one for Dad, too. I only have this one left; this is a special one."

Chelsea's mother seemed surprised. "Oh. Well,

I think I have some scraps of lace in my sewing basket.''

Chelsea got out the glue and stuck two rows of white lace all around the outside of the red heart. Then, in fancy cursive, with curling capital letters, she wrote, ''To Arthur, Love and Kisses, from—''

Mrs. Martin put her hand on Chelsea's arm. ''Are you going to sign it?''

''Uh...'' Chelsea looked at her mother. ''Why?''

''Well,'' Mrs. Martin hesitated. ''Sometimes, when someone sends a valentine like that, he or she signs it, 'From Your Secret Admirer.'''

''Oh,'' said Chelsea, considering the matter. ''So the person who's getting the valentine doesn't know for sure who sent it? Okay.''

Being a secret admirer would be sort of exciting. And if Arthur didn't like the card...well, she was sure he *would* like it.

When the third grade came into school on February fourteenth, everyone discovered white paper bags, decorated with red hearts. Overnight they had mysteriously appeared on the desks.

"Mrs. Findlay did it," said Mary Lynne. "We're supposed to put the valentines in them."

Chelsea glanced at her teacher. Mrs. Findlay was wearing a long-sleeved red dress and red high heels. A little gold heart was pinned to her collar.

This is going to be a perfect day, thought Chelsea. And she couldn't wait to see what Arthur thought of his valentine.

Back and forth across the room she went, dropping a small, white envelope into each bag. Now she was glad she had a card for everyone. And she was saving Arthur's extra-special, extra-large valentine for last.

She pulled the red heart from a plastic bag. It was so big she had to bend it a little to fit it into Arthur's valentine bag.

"What's that?" demanded Thomas, who sat next to Arthur.

"What?" said Chelsea, jumping a little. Thomas had startled her. She hurried back to her seat, feeling slightly uneasy.

At two o'clock, it was time for the Valentine's

Day party. "You may open your cards now," announced Mrs. Findlay. Immediately, the room was filled with the sound of ripping paper.

Chelsea opened her cards slowly, trying to make them last a long time. All the while, she kept an eye on Arthur. She smiled to herself, imagining the look on his face when he saw her card.

Her thoughts were interrupted by a loud squawk, as if an angry parrot had found its way into the classroom. Oh, no! It was Arthur. Scowling, he held her valentine up for the class to see.

"Who sent me this mushy stuff?" he demanded. "I'm gonna kill 'em!"

Chelsea's heart began to thump. Arthur was not reacting at all the way she had imagined he would.

The other boys crowded around Arthur's desk, begging, "Let me see! Let me see!"

Mrs. Findlay clapped her hands. "Get back to your seats, boys!"

In the moment of silence that followed, only Thomas's voice could be heard. "It was Chelsea," he called out. "Chelsea sent it!"

Chelsea shrank down in her seat, feeling everyone's eyes on her. This was not one bit romantic!

She was glad to see that Mrs. Findlay and the room mother, Mrs. Klein, were passing out the party food. Three heart-shaped cookies apiece, two Hershey's kisses, and a cup of red Hawaiian Punch. That would distract the boys.

Chelsea glanced at Arthur. He had settled back in his seat and was stuffing a cookie into his mouth. On the floor, beside his desk, was the big red heart, all crumpled.

"Psst," whispered Mary Lynne. "Did you really send Arthur that card?"

"Who, *me*?" answered Chelsea.

I guess it's not the right time yet for me to fall in love, she told herself forlornly. She glared at Arthur. And he was definitely not the right person.

He might be the tallest boy in the third grade, but he was also the rudest. And besides. . . he had dirty ears!

···10···

Too Much Fun

Chelsea stared out the window of the airplane. Wispy-looking clouds made shadows on the ground below. There was no school on Monday, in honor of Presidents' Day, and she was on her way to visit her father.

Pushing a cart filled with refreshments, a flight attendant came down the aisle. Chelsea chose a lemon-lime soda.

She took a sip, then set her drink down on the fold-out tray table. After searching in her tote bag, she pulled out a book.

She studied the cover. On it was a picture of a girl. But not just any girl.

This girl had long, reddish braids hanging over her shoulders and a wide-brimmed straw hat perched on the back of her head. A carpet-bag sat on her lap. This girl was Anne of Green Gables.

Chelsea and her mother had watched the television series about Anne. Later, when Chelsea saw the book in the library, she wanted to read it. But *Anne of Green Gables* is a difficult book for a third-grader.

"I'm going to visit my dad," she told the librarian. "He'll help me with it."

Now she snuggled back in her seat. Sipping her drink, she stared at the book cover and then out the window.

It seemed like no time at all before the captain was announcing their arrival. Because she was traveling alone, Chelsea had to stay seated until everyone else left the plane.

Then the flight attendant introduced her to a smiling young woman. She was an airline agent who would take Chelsea to the terminal to find her father.

"Have a nice visit!" said the flight attendant.

Chelsea waved goodbye. Then she started down the passage between the airplane and the building.

"Wait for me!" Miss Morrison, the airline agent, laughed. "I guess you're in a hurry to see your father, aren't you?"

Chelsea smiled and nodded. Soon she was standing with Miss Morrison in the terminal, staring about her.

Everywhere were crowds of people. But where was her dad? For a moment Chelsea felt a terrible doubt. Mr. Martin was a little absent-minded; but surely, he wouldn't forget to meet her plane. Would he?

Then she heard his voice. "Chelsea! Over here!"

She started to run and then slowed to a walk. That smiling man was her father, yes, but he looked *different*.

"Chelsea!" he cried, and gave her a hug. She hugged him back and introduced him to Miss Morrison. While her dad signed an identification paper, Chelsea tried not to stare. There was something wrong with the lower part of his face.

In a little while, Chelsea and her father were alone. She reached up to touch his chin. "Daddy, what's this?"

Mr. Martin laughed. "Oh, that's right. You haven't seen it yet. I'm growing a beard."

He ran his hand over his chin. "You like it?"

Chelsea frowned, thinking about all the times in the past few months she had talked to her dad on the telephone. She had pictured him looking just the way she had seen him last. And that picture had been wrong!

Her father noticed the frown. "Uh-oh, I guess you *don't* like it."

Now she felt a little uncomfortable. She didn't want to hurt his feelings. And it wasn't that she disliked beards. But she wanted everything about him to stay the same. Always.

Mr. Martin drew a circle in the air. "Turn around and let me take a look at you."

Why did he want her to do that? she wondered, as she spun about. There wasn't anything different about *her.*

Her father said, "Hmmm, your hair is longer."

Chelsea was surprised. "Do you think so?" She twisted her neck around, trying to see if somehow, without her knowing it, her hair had crept past her shoulders.

"And you've gotten taller, that's for sure." Her father's expression turned serious, even sad.

Mr. Martin sighed. "My little girl is growing up."

She didn't think she had grown *that* much. Compared to a lot of third-graders, she was small. "Well...," she said slowly, "I have to grow, don't I?"

Her father laughed. "Yes, I guess you're right." He turned and headed toward the baggage pickup area. "Let's go get your suitcase."

In a crowd of people, they stood waiting as the luggage went round and round on a conveyor belt. Finally, Chelsea's small, rather battered blue case appeared.

In the car on the way to her father's apartment, Chelsea had a sudden, dismaying thought. "Dad! Is there a big sale at the store on Monday? You don't have to work, do you?''

Mr. Martin was the manager of the hardware department at Sears. Sometimes he had to work when everyone else was having a holiday.

But her father shook his head. ''Mike, the assistant manager, is going to handle it. I have the whole weekend off!''

They made a sharp right turn, and Chelsea's tote bag fell over on her feet. That reminded her of the book, *Anne of Green Gables*, inside it. ''Daddy,'' she said. ''There's something I want—''

Just then her father turned into a driveway. ''Here we are, Chelsea!''

She forgot about the book. There was the big, old, white-painted house! Mr. Martin lived on the second floor. A wooden stairway on the outside of the house led to his apartment.

Soon they were standing in front of his door. ''Here we go.'' He pulled out his key and unlocked it.

Chelsea stepped inside. Nothing's changed, she thought, noticing a dirty sock in the middle of the floor. The apartment had the same air of comfortable sloppiness that she remembered.

She sniffed the air. The apartment smelled the same, too. Turning to her father, she said, "You had pizza for breakfast, didn't you, Dad?"

"We-ell, yes." Mr. Martin seemed embarrassed. "There's nothing wrong with pizza. It's a perfectly healthy food."

After unpacking, Chelsea went into the living room. Looking around, she discovered something *had* changed.

She turned to her father. "You've got a new chair!"

"Uh-huh. Sit in it and see what it can do."

Chelsea sat. Her father pressed a lever, and her feet and legs were lifted into the air.

"See?" said Mr. Martin. "It's a recliner."

Chelsea stroked the soft blue seat cover. Why, she thought, this chair was practically big enough for two people sitting together. And that reminded her of something.

She picked up her tote bag and took out *Anne of Green Gables*. I'll ask Dad to read it right now, she thought. But then she discovered he was no longer in the room.

Looking in the hallway, she was surprised to see that her father had put on his overcoat. And he was carrying her own pink parka over his arm.

"Let's go, honey," he said.

"Are we going out for lunch?"

He held her coat up by the shoulders. "Yes, and we're going other places, too. I've got lots of plans for this weekend."

Chelsea was surprised. Her father didn't usually make a lot of plans. Usually they just did whatever they felt like doing at the time. They played Monopoly or Scrabble, watched videos, or went shopping at the mall where her father worked.

"You mean we're not coming back here after lunch?" she asked.

"That's right. After lunch we're going to—" her father took a small piece of paper out of his pocket and looked at it "—to the art museum."

Chelsea thought about Anne of Green Gables, with her red braids hanging over her shoulders. "But—"

"No *buts*," said her father. "You'll see, we'll have fun."

Oh well, thought Chelsea. She loved drawing pictures. Probably, she *would* like the art museum. And later her father would read the book to her.

It was dark when they returned. After touring the museum, they had been just in time for the late afternoon showing of a Walt Disney movie.

Then, they'd gone out for pizza. Chelsea thought her father could never get too much pizza. This time they had ordered the Supreme Pizza Feast, with ten different toppings. It was so big that even her father had not been able to finish it.

"Did you have fun, Chelsea?" he asked, as he put a cardboard box of leftover pizza in the refrigerator.

"Uh-huh." Chelsea yawned and plopped down on the plaid sofa.

She was still holding the bag from the art museum gift shop. All afternoon, she had carried it around. Now she opened it and admired the gifts her father had bought for her—a small box of colored pencils and a dinosaur-shaped pad of paper.

Later, sitting in her pajamas and sipping chocolate milk, she decided she would draw a picture before she went to bed.

There was a painting in the museum she liked, of pink and white flowers—peonies—in a vase. She thought she would try to draw something like that.

Uh-oh, the blue pencil, her favorite, was missing!

She searched between the sofa cushions, but it wasn't there. Getting down on her hands and knees, she reached under the sofa. Yes, here was her pencil.

But...oo-o-oh! What was this other thing? Quickly, she snatched back her hand.

She had touched something flat and stiff. And a little bit...sticky?

She peered into the darkness. Then, gingerly, pulled something out. "Da-ad, what's this?" Between her thumb and forefinger, she held a dusty brown rectangle.

"Oh!" Mr. Martin looked sheepish. He came closer. "I think," he said, examining it, "I think that's a peanut butter and jelly sandwich." Then he added, "or...it used to be, anyway."

"Are you *sure*?" Chelsea dropped the disgusting object into her father's hand.

"Yes, that's right. I remember now. I made a sandwich when I was watching the late show. That must be the half I didn't eat."

"But how did it get under the sofa?"

Mr. Martin shrugged. "I don't know, Chelsea. These things happen..." He tossed the sandwich in a wastepaper basket.

"But, I do know it's time for you to get to bed." He gave her a kiss. "Now, scoot!"

At seven in the morning, the alarm clock went *beep...beep...beep*! Chelsea opened her eyes and stared at the unfamiliar ceiling. Then she remembered—she was visiting her father.

She discovered that she was hungry and headed for the kitchen.

Soon she was sitting at the table, eating Cheerios with milk. Her father was across from her, sipping Orange & Spice Tea, and turning the pages of a large, flat, soft-bound book.

All at once, she noticed what kind of book it was. She sat up straight. "Daddy, why are you looking at a book of street maps?" Even as the words came out of her mouth, Chelsea realized the answer. They were going somewhere again.

Mr. Martin looked up and smiled. "Did you know, Chelsea, that there is an ice-skating rink right here?"

He stuck his finger on the map. "Only half an hour's drive away. And they even rent out skates."

"But, Daddy. . ." Chelsea thought of *Anne of Green Gables*, sitting on a table in the living room. When would they have a chance to read it?

A crease appeared between her father's eyebrows. "But what? You like going places, don't you? You had a good time yesterday."

Feeling helpless, Chelsea nodded. She had to agree. She did like going places. But not all the time.

She didn't want to interfere with his plans,

but she had plans, too. Today she thought she would really rather stay home.

She decided to try once more. "Daddy, I don't even know how to ice skate!"

"Nothing to it," said her father. "We have some errands to do, and then we'll go ice skating. You'll get the hang of it in no time."

They did a little grocery shopping, took Mr. Martin's shirts to the laundry, and returned some books to the library. Then they stopped for gas.

By this time, Chelsea was hungry again. She saw a doughnut shop and convinced her father to stop.

"Hmmm," said Mr. Martin. "I wonder if they have pizza-flavored doughnuts."

"*Daddy*!" said Chelsea.

Mr. Martin laughed. "Just kidding!"

They ordered oatmeal-raisin muffins and milk. While they waited, Mr. Martin glanced at a newspaper. "Hey," he said, "here's another good movie. Do you want to see it before we go ice skating?"

Chelsea hesitated. This was turning out to be

an awfully busy day! But...she *did* want to see the movie.

Three hours later, they arrived at the ice-skating rink. Right away, things began to go wrong.

"We don't have skates your size," said the girl behind the counter to Mr. Martin. "The best we can do is one size larger."

"Maybe we should go home," Chelsea suggested.

"No, no, these will be just fine," said Mr. Martin.

To her surprise, Chelsea found that ice skating was not terribly different from roller skating. Although she slipped twice, she was soon able to glide slowly around the rink. She even began to enjoy herself.

But then she noticed her father! He was tottering about in his too-large skates, a very worried look on his face.

Uh-oh, Chelsea thought, I can't stand to watch! She scrunched up her eyes.

A few seconds later, she heard a *crash*!—and then a moan. She opened her eyes. There was her father, flat on his back on the hard ice.

"Daddy! Are you all right?"

"Chelsea," said Mr. Martin, after she helped him up, "it's time to go home."

He spent the evening lying on the sofa, an electric heating pad under his back. Chelsea sat nearby, drawing with her new pencils and watching television. For dinner, they had leftover pizza.

The next morning, the alarm clock went *beep ...beep...beep.* Chelsea opened her eyes and looked around. This time she remembered exactly where she was. She tiptoed into the hallway.

Except for the ticking of the clock, the apartment was silent. She peeked around the corner into the kitchen. And there was her father, siting at the table. He was awake all right, and he must be feeling better.

At least, she thought he was awake. But his head was cradled in his arms. "Daddy!" she whispered.

He lifted his head. "Oh...Chelsea." He yawned and rubbed his eyes. "You're up early."

Then Chelsea noticed the book of street maps

was open in front of him. Oh, no! Not again. Not after yesterday!

Aloud, she said, "Are we going somewhere today?"

"Bowling."

"Oh." Chelsea began to pour orange juice into a glass.

She sat down across from her father. His elbow was on the table, his hand propping up his face. She had the feeling that if his hand weren't there, his head would fall right down onto the table.

"Daddy," said Chelsea, "you look kind of tired."

"Not at all," he said, as he slowly flipped the pages of the map book.

Chelsea took a deep breath. This is my last chance, she thought. My last day here. "Daddy?"

"Yes?"

Her words tumbled out in a rush. "I don't want to go bowling."

"You don't?"

She shook her head. "I'm tired of going

places, and there's a book I want you to read. It's too hard for me. And I want to play Scrabble!''

Slowly he reached out and closed the book of street maps. Chelsea held her breath. Was he angry?

No, he was smiling. ''Good! I don't want to go bowling, either.''

He winked at Chelsea. ''After all, I barely survived ice skating yesterday!''

The microwave went *ding*! Mr. Martin opened it and removed a paper plate containing the last slice of leftover pizza.

''Daddy,'' said Chelsea, ''I don't understand. Why were you planning a bowling trip if you didn't want to go bowling?''

''We-ell, it was because of you, Chelsea.''

''What do you mean?''

''My friend Mike took his kids to Disney World over Christmas vacation. And I thought... well, I just wanted us to have fun!''

''Oh!'' Chelsea thought about it. ''It *was* fun, Daddy. But maybe it was too much fun. For one weekend, I mean.''

After breakfast they sat on the living room floor and played two games of Scrabble. Mr. Martin won, but as he explained, that was because he knew more words.

"Do you want to play again?" he asked.

Chelsea shook her head. She went to the table and picked up *Anne of Green Gables*. "Will you read this to me?" Grasping her father's hand, she dragged him over to the new blue chair.

"Are you sure we'll both fit?" asked Mr. Martin.

Chelsea nodded. But it turned out they were kind of squished.

She pulled the lever on the side of the chair. The bottom of the chair went up, and now their feet were almost level with their heads.

This is nice, she thought. Not quite comfortable but nice all the same. She handed her father the book.

"*Anne of Green Gables*," he began. "Chapter One."

Mary Lynne and Chelsea

It was Saturday morning, and Mary Lynne had come over to play. Chelsea took a grocery bag out of her bedroom closet. "Here are the doll clothes. See if you can find something to fit Susan, okay?"

She picked up the blonde-haired doll by the leg and passed it to Mary Lynne. "A dress, maybe."

Mary Lynne pulled doll-sized skirts, tops, and dresses one by one from the bag. "Nope. . .no. . . too small. . .too big. . .what's this? Oh, it's a comb for a doll."

Mary Lynne dropped the clothes onto the

floor. "I know, let's fix her hair first."

"Okay." Chelsea opened a desk drawer and took out a plastic bag full of pudgy pink hair rollers. "These were Mom's, but she doesn't use them anymore."

Mary Lynne examined the rollers. She squeezed one between her thumb and forefinger, let go, and watched it spring back into shape. "Hey, I like these. Why doesn't your mother want them?"

In her lap, Chelsea held another doll, Stephanie, who had long, brown hair. She gripped Stephanie's legs between her knees and used both hands to wind some hair on a roller. "Well, she doesn't need them now. She has a style called 'wash-and-wear.'"

Mary Lynne fastened a roller onto the head of the doll named Susan. "Wash-and-wear sounds like a shirt or something." She giggled, letting go of the pink roller. Immediately, it fell out. "Hey, this isn't working."

Chelsea had already finished three curls. Now she stopped and looked at her friend. "Maybe we should wet her hair."

Mary Lynne shook her head. "It just isn't

long enough to wrap around the roller." She shrugged and began to tell Chelsea about a hair style she'd seen in one of her mother's magazines.

Chelsea looked down at Stephanie in her lap. She felt a little guilty for taking the doll with the longest hair, when her friend had short-haired Susan.

She remembered a television commercial she'd seen that morning. "It would be nice if Susan was the kind of doll with hair that grows."

"Yeah, but she's not."

Chelsea stared at the doll's head. "Hey, let me see her a minute."

She pointed to Susan's bubble-gum colored scalp. "See how her hair comes out of her head in little bunches? I think I know how to make doll hair grow!"

"You do?" Mary Lynne seemed doubtful. "How?"

"We-e-ell, I think there's a lot of hair all balled up inside her head." Chelsea pressed lightly on Susan's scalp. "If you pull *real* hard, it comes out."

Mary Lynne reached over and snatched Susan out of Chelsea's hands. "Like this?" She grabbed a handful of doll hair and yanked.

"Oh!" gasped Chelsea.

Looking very surprised, Mary Lynne stared at the large section of doll hair that had come off in her hand. "It didn't work," she said slowly.

Then she giggled. "Sor-ry! Hey, I'm pretty strong, aren't I?"

Without a word, Chelsea picked up Susan. She was so angry she couldn't talk. She walked over to her toy chest, opened it, and threw the doll in.

Mary Lynne looked at her, wide-eyed. "Hey, are you mad?"

Chelsea pressed her lips together and shook her head. She felt, somehow, that she was not being fair. It *was* her idea. But...she hadn't expected Mary Lynne to actually try it.

Mary Lynne went to the toy chest and took out Susan. "It's not that bad," she said, studying the doll's hair. "It reminds me of the time I cut some of *my* hair, when I was little."

She giggled. "It was only *this* long," she said, measuring two inches in the air with her thumb and forefinger. "My mom was so mad! And I had to get all my hair cut really short."

She stared at Chelsea. Chelsea stared back.

Then Chelsea nodded. "Okay, let's do it." In her desk she found a pair of scissors. "But I don't want it to be *too* short."

Mary Lynne arranged the doll so that she was sitting upright on the floor. "Now, where are the scissors?"

Chelsea set them on the floor next to the doll. "Just a minute—I'll go find a towel to put around her shoulders."

In a few moments she returned with a wash-cloth. "Maybe this will work for—" she began. Then she stood still and stared at the scene before her. Mary Lynne was kneeling over the doll, the scissors in her hand.

Hey, wait a minute, Chelsea thought.

Snip! Snip! The scissors flashed. Mary Lynne cut one side of Susan's hair.

Chelsea rushed forward. Snip! Snip! Before

she could stop her, Mary Lynne chopped off the other side!

"Okay," said Mary Lynne. "Now I'll style it."

Chelsea stood still, watching. Her face felt funny, as if it were frozen. *I* wanted to cut Susan's hair, she thought. She's *my* doll!

Mary Lynne hummed as she worked. Snip! Snip! "How about bangs?"

Chelsea felt too angry to answer. But Mary Lynne didn't seem to notice. She just went right on cutting.

For the next half-hour Chelsea ignored Mary Lynne. She dressed Stephanie and set her in the doll-sized high chair. She set a small plastic fork and a plastic dish of bacon and eggs in front of her.

"Okay now, eat your breakfast like a good girl," she told Stephanie.

At last Mary Lynne was finished with Susan. She held her up for Chelsea to see. "There! How does that look?"

But Chelsea didn't answer. She acted as if Mary Lynne weren't even there. "Okay, eat some more," she said to Stephanie. She would talk to the doll but *not* to Mary Lynne.

Mary Lynne shrugged. Soon she stood up. "I think it's time for me to go home for lunch."

Chelsea walked to the door with her. "Goodbye," said Mary Lynne. "See you on Monday!" She grinned at Chelsea, but Chelsea didn't smile back.

"Is anything wrong?" Mary Lynne added uncertainly.

"No," muttered Chelsea, staring at her shoe. "Goodbye."

Mary Lynne shrugged, waved, and skipped off down the front walk.

Chelsea closed the door. She felt like kicking it. She *would* kick it. Ow! She hopped around, holding her foot. Now she felt even worse.

She opened the door again and then—*bang!*—slammed it shut. There! Take that, Mary Lynne Woodlie!

By Monday morning, though, Chelsea had forgiven her. What could she do? she asked herself. She didn't want to lose her best friend.

But being best friends with Mary Lynne was like being on a roller coaster, up one minute and down the next. Why does she act the way she does sometimes? thought Chelsea, sighing. Why can't she just do what I want her to do?

At least this would be a good morning at school. After math came art class, one of her favorite subjects. And then the once-a-week computer class. For days, she'd been looking forward to using the *Paint Show* program.

Of course, at the beginning of the year, she and Mary Lynne had chosen each other as partners. Now they pulled their chairs close together.

"I'll go first," said Mary Lynne. She moved the mouse around on the table, and soon the head of a pig-tailed girl appeared on the screen.

Chelsea glanced at the big clock on the wall. Mary Lynne had ten more minutes, then it was her turn.

"Whoops!" said Mary Lynne, giggling. "Her arms are too short, but I'll fix that."

Five more minutes, thought Chelsea. Mary Lynne drew the picture, but I'll get to fill it in.

She started to imagine how the pig-tailed girl would look with black hair. Maybe she should make it orange. Or even purple!

Mrs. Findlay clapped her hands, making her gold bracelets jingle. "All right, class, it's time to switch places."

Chelsea half stood up, preparing to scoot her chair closer to the computer. But Mary Lynne was staring at the screen. She didn't move.

Chelsea leaned closer. "Mary Lynne!"

Mary Lynne stretched out one hand, as if to push Chelsea away. "Wait a minute—I have to get her feet right."

Chelsea sank back down on her chair and glanced at the clock. That's two minutes of my time she's taken, she said to herself.

Mary Lynne concentrated on the computer screen. "No...no, that's still not right." She worked another couple of minutes in silence. Finally, she seemed satisfied with her work. "There! Pretty good, don't you think?"

"Mmmm," murmured Chelsea. At last, she told herself. My turn.

But then, instead of standing up to give Chelsea her seat, Mary Lynne began to fill in the girl's clothes with a pattern of stripes. "How do you like this purple and yellow for her shirt?" she asked.

Oh, no! thought Chelsea, ignoring Mary Lynne's question. She's doing it again—she's not going to let me even have a turn. She's going to use up our entire computer-class time all by herself!

And that was just what Mary Lynne did.

···12···

Chelsea's Turn

It was recess that same morning, and Chelsea was standing in line for the tire swing.

Glumly, she watched as Paula and Lucy Burnett did a hand clap. "*S-O, S-O. . .S-O-S!*" they sang. "*My mother, your mother, live in the West.*"
Every night they have a fight
And this is what they say tonight.
Boys are rotten, made of cotton!
Girls are dandy, made of candy!

Katie Klein turned to Chelsea and held up her hands, palms out. "Come on—let's do *Miss Mary Mack*."

But Chelsea shook her head.

"What's the *matter* with you?" asked Katie.

"Nothing," muttered Chelsea.

Katie shrugged. "You sure look like something's the matter."

Chelsea tried to keep from scowling, but it was no use. Everything was the matter! She felt terrible, and it was all the fault of Mary Lynne Woodlie.

Beverly Ann came running up. "Mind if I squeeze in here in front of you, Chelsea?"

Without even thinking, Chelsea said, "Yes, I do mind." She stepped closer to Katie so there was no room for the other girl.

"Humph!" Beverly Ann flipped her long hair over her shoulder and went to the end of the line.

"She has a lot of nerve!" said a voice. It was Mary Lynne—the last person Chelsea wanted to see right now.

"You'd think *she* was your best friend," Mary Lynne went on. She began to push between Katie and Chelsea. "Hey, give me some room!"

Chelsea glared at her. Then she took a deep breath. I don't *care* if she gets mad and won't be my best friend anymore, she thought.

"Ma-ry Lynne," she said clearly. "You can *not* get in front of me."

Mary Lynne gave her a blank look. "Why not?"

Oo-o-oh! Chelsea felt like screaming. Hey, what if she did? What if she just opened her mouth as wide as she possibly could and let out a yell? No, not a yell...a shriek. An ear-piercing, glass-shattering scream!

She imagined the shocked look on Mary Lynne's face. And, in spite of her anger, she couldn't help smiling.

"Oh, good," Mary Lynne said. "I thought for a minute you were mad at me."

Chelsea couldn't believe it. Didn't Mary Lynne *know* that she was angry with her? Aloud, she said, "Of course I'm mad at you!"

Mary Lynne looked puzzled. "But why?"

Oh, boy! thought Chelsea. She acts as if she didn't do anything. Again she glared at Mary Lynne. "I'm mad at you for lots of reasons—like cutting Susan's hair on Saturday. She's my doll, and I wanted to do it.''

Mary Lynne stared back, clearly astonished. ''Why didn't you say so, then? You didn't tell me to stop.''

''Why didn't I *say* so?'' Chelsea repeated. ''You should have *known*—''

Mary Lynne's eyebrows went up, and her big brown eyes widened. ''I don't think that's fair!'' she said. ''You didn't tell me I was doing something you didn't like. You just got mad at me!''

Chelsea stuck her fingers in her ears and squeezed her eyes shut. She didn't want to hear what Mary Lynne was saying.

She began to talk rapidly. ''Today, in computer class, you hogged the *Paint Show* program, and I never got a chance to do anything!''

She stopped for a second, took a deep breath, and went on. ''And just now, you wanted to shove in line ahead of me, and I've been waiting for my turn ever since recess started!''

''Oh!'' Mary Lynne looked guilty.

Chelsea took her fingers out of her ears.

''Well, sor-ry!'' said Mary Lynne. ''But I

can't read your mind. If you don't actually *say* something, I just go ahead and do what I want to do.'' She shrugged. ''I'm just used to it, I guess.''

Chelsea stared at her friend. This was a new idea. Maybe even someone who's quiet, like me, she thought, has to speak up sometimes.

She turned to Mary Lynne. ''You mean, you really didn't know how I felt? You didn't know you were making me mad?''

''Well, you were acting funny, so I guessed you were unhappy about something. I just didn't know it was me.''

Mary Lynne picked a blade of grass and twirled it between her fingers. ''Uh...are you still mad?''

''Well,'' said Chelsea, ''I think I should get to use the computer the whole time next week. It's only fair!''

''Uh...okay.'' Mary Lynne's mouth turned down.

''Are you *still* mad?''

Hey, thought Chelsea, now she's worried about *my* being angry. And I had always worried about *her* being angry! From now on, I'm going to tell her what's bothering me. She's my best friend, after all.

Chelsea shook her head and smiled. "No, I'm not mad."

"Well, come on, then." Mary Lynne tugged at her arm. "It's your turn on the tire swing!"

BECKY THOMAN LINDBERG lives in Baltimore, Maryland, with her husband, son, and daughter, as well as a dog, two cats, and a rabbit. Besides writing, she enjoys art; she paints landscapes and portraits in oils and pastel.

As a child, Mrs. Lindberg read many books and occasionally wrote stories of her own. *Speak Up, Chelsea Martin!* is her first book. It was inspired by her childhood memories and by the adventures of her daughter, Carolyn. Mrs. Lindberg also believes that everyone should learn to "speak up"— in a nice way, of course.